When Secrets *Come* Home

GATLIN FIELDS

Sandra Waggoner

Sable Creek
PRESS

Cover and text design by Diane King, www.dkingdesigner.com
Maggie photo by Deb Minnard; model Amanda Sheppard
Cover photo of barn © Mmm Eee | Dreamstime.com
Back cover photo © istockphoto.com | Aurelian Gogonea

Scripture taken from the King James Version. Public domain.

Published by Sable Creek Press, PO Box 12217, Glendale, Arizona 85318
www.sablecreekpress.com

Publisher's Cataloging-in-Publication data

Waggoner, Sandra.
    When secrets come home / Sandra Waggoner.
        p. cm.
        "Gatlin Fields"
        Summary: A dangerous intruder, working for her enemy, and heaping coals of kindness help Maggie Daniels appreciate her new family and to trust God more.
        ISBN 9780976682318

[1. Depressions—1929—Kansas—Fiction. 2. Family life—Kansas—Fiction. 3. Fathers and daughters—Fiction. 4. Christian fiction.] I. Title.
PZ7.W124135. In 2010
[Fic]—dc22

                                                                2010921011
Printed in the United States of America.

Chapters

CHAPTER 1

Spear in the Night

Maggie lay silently as tears rolled down her face. She swiped them away with her hand.

"It's okay to cry," Opal whispered.

Maggie drew in her breath. She had thought the girls were asleep.

Opal stroked Maggie's arm soothingly. "It was your mama's birthday. It's okay to cry."

Maggie rolled over and lay on her back. "How did you know?"

"Mama told me. She said we should be especially nice to you today."

Ruby cut in, "I didn't know that."

"That's 'cause you would blab," Opal informed Ruby.

"I would not." Ruby stuck out her bottom lip.

Maggie smiled. She liked her new sisters.

"Here, Maggie. You can put this on just for tonight. It will make you feel better." Opal slipped the chain from around her neck and pressed it into Maggie's hand.

"Why?"

Opal scrunched beneath the cool sheet. "It just will."

"Does it hold special magic?"

Ruby rolled over to rest her chin in her hands. "Opal thinks it does. She won't even let me touch it."

Opal jabbed Ruby. "Not with your grubby old hands. Besides, you'd probably lose it."

"I would not!"

Maggie could feel Ruby glaring in the darkness.

"Would, too!" Opal hissed.

"Would not!"

Maggie interrupted before a fight could rage. "Just tell me why it's so special." She held high the gold chain from which a key dangled.

Opal reached over and pressed the key to her lips. "Mama gave it to me. Daddy gave it to her. He told her it was the key to his heart and all the secrets it held."

"You sure it's okay for me to wear it?" Maggie asked.

"Yep, but just for tonight."

"Maggie can wear it, but not me?" Ruby sat up in bed.

"Just for tonight, Ruby!" Opal whispered.

"Thanks, Opal. Just for tonight." Maggie closed her hand about the chain.

Ruby grabbed the sheet and yanked it. "That's not fair!"

"Hey!" Opal began.

"Opal, Ruby, both of you go to sleep. You don't want your mama coming, do you?" Maggie warned. "Ruby, turn toward the wall. Opal, turn toward me. Both of you go to sleep."

Ruby, still mumbling, scooted as close to the wall as she could.

Maggie turned to face the window. She listened to the sounds of the boxcar slip into sleep. The soft wind hummed through the screened porch. A branch caressed the side of the house. An owl hooted from the giant cottonwood in the pasture. On the other side of the boxcar, Daddy's snores comforted her. Maggie felt the tension ease from Ruby as she sank away from the wall. Opal's warm breath tickled Maggie's neck. Maggie pulled the sheet over her head until only her eyes peeked out. Today had been her mama's birthday, her real mama, not Sue. Every chance she had, Maggie had watched Daddy to see if he remembered, but she couldn't tell. She hadn't asked him because if he didn't remember, she didn't want to remind him. Always before when her mama's birthday rolled around, Daddy had told her. He would tell her about Mama's first birthday after they were married, and how he had tried to make her a cake. He said it had tasted more like frosted cornbread than cake, and it was about an inch tall. Daddy told her that Mama hadn't cared. They had laughed together and had eaten the whole thing! Each year after that, Daddy would make Mama a cake. Maggie remembered the cakes. Daddy had gotten better until he became a really good cake maker. That first birthday after Mama died was hard. Maggie had awakened to the smell of cake baking in the oven, and had gotten out of bed and slipped down the stairs. She saw Daddy slumped with his head on the table where he hadn't yet cleared away the mixing bowl, flour, sugar and the other ingredients. As Maggie looked at him, she thought really his broken heart lay there.

Remembering, Maggie swallowed a sob, slid out of bed and sank to the floor by the window. She gazed up at the moon. It was a "sliver" moon, the kind Mama had called a smiley moon.

Mama would laugh and say, "Smiley moon, you're up too soon, the sun's still in the sky. Across your face, the wild geese race. Against winter's wind they southward fly."

Maggie laid her arms along the windowsill and rested her chin. Her fingers found Opal's gold chain and stroked the key. She wished it did hold magic. She could sure use some to fight all the memories that flooded her being. Would everything remind her of Mama? It didn't hurt as much as it used to. Time helped, and Sue helped. Sue had been the best person in the whole world to be a mama for Maggie and a wife for Daddy. Maggie didn't regret Daddy marrying Sue. Maggie sighed. Somewhere up there in heaven, Mama was with God. She didn't have to worry about this horrible depression, or where Daddy would find a job, or if he would find a job. Mama didn't have to worry about Maggie working with Mrs. Crenshaw. Mama didn't have to worry about Daddy losing the farm. Mama didn't have a worry in the world.

"Dear God up in heaven, please tell my mama happy birthday and that I love her and miss her so much!"

A flutter of wings broke into Maggie's whispers. She pulled her eyes from the distant skies. It must have been the owl from the cottonwood swooping down on its supper for tonight.

Dry grass crunched. A shiver rolled across Maggie's back. Something was out there. She rubbed her eyes and searched the dark. Nothing. She let out her breath. It must have been Lulubelle. Yes. It had to have been Lulubelle. The night was too quiet, and she must have been imagining things. Still, she listened. Opal's gentle snores and Ruby's quiet breathing eased her mind. It was late and morning would come all too soon. She stood and turned from the window.

CLANK!

Maggie froze. Her heart began surging forth to win whatever race it was running. Slowly, making no sound, she turned back to the window. She listened. She put her hand over her heart to settle it down. If her heart were quiet, she might be better able to hear.

CLANK!

She swallowed. That was not Lulubelle!

CLANK!

She scanned the dark. The only light came from the sliver moon, but the sound seemed to be coming from the lean-to where the horses and Lulubelle stayed. On bare feet, Maggie slipped to their quilted bedroom door, eased through it and let the quilt fall back into place. She edged to the outside door and grasped the cold knob in her hand. Maggie paused to whisper a prayer. "Please, don't squeak." Slowly she pushed the door and slid past it. The porch creaked with each step, and to Maggie it sounded like drums. At the screen door, Maggie gritted her teeth. She twisted the piece of one-by-two that made a locking latch, held her breath and inched through the door. Silently, she stood on the steps and listened.

CLANK!

The noise definitely came from the lean-to, but it did not seem to bother the animals, so it must not be anything for her to fear. Maggie went down the steps and headed toward the lean-to. As she got closer, she saw Lulubelle swish her tail, and both horses snoozing. She looked around the lean-to. Nothing. She must have heard the wind carrying noise from further away than she had thought. She sighed and turned to head back to the house.

CLANK!

Maggie froze. The noise came from behind the barn.

CLANK!

"What's this?" Someone was back there.

CLANK!

"Of all the …"

Maggie stayed in the shadows and made her way to the lean-to side. She took a deep breath, pressed herself against the wall, and edged around to the back of the shed. She peeked out just enough to see a man digging with a shovel against the rugged foundation of the lean-to. Maggie sighed with relief. It was Daddy! That was why the noise didn't worry Lulubelle and the horses a bit. Maggie stepped out and smiled. "Daddy, what are you doing?"

The man twisted and turned. "Who's there?" Swiftly he raised the shovel like a spear and flung it at Maggie.

She felt the wind as the shovel whistled by her head. Maggie had no time to think as she belly-busted the ground and clawed at the dry grass, trying to get her footing. She half crawled as she stumbled into a death run toward the house. She broke through the doors of the porch and the boxcar, slid across the floor, yanked open the cardboard covered screened door of her mama and daddy's bedroom, and jumped in the middle between them.

Sue screamed.

Daddy grabbed Maggie and relaxed as he realized who she was. "Maggie!"

Sue was still breathing hard. "Maggie?"

Opal and Ruby plunged into the bedroom, eyes wide.

"Maggie, are you all right?" Daddy asked.

"I- I- I thought he was you!" Maggie stuttered.

"Who, Maggie?" Daddy spoke quietly.

Maggie swallowed. "There was a man out behind the cow shed. He had a shovel, and he was digging. He was in the shadows, and I thought he was you. When I called to him, he turned around and threw the shovel at me! He threw it just like a spear!"

"Are you sure Maggie?" Sue held her throat.

"Why were you outside?" Daddy wanted to know.

"Maybe it was a dream," Opal added.

"It was not a dream. I heard a noise, and I went outside to see what it was." Maggie was still in her daddy's arms, just where she wanted to be.

Gently her daddy scolded, "Maggie, never go outside like that again. If you hear something, you come and get me. Do you understand?"

Maggie nodded.

Daddy wiped away the tears Maggie didn't even know she had shed. "Let me go check things out."

Sue looked long at Daddy. "Girls, let's go warm some milk."

The girls went to the table, and Sue poured milk into a pan. No one said a word. Daddy walked through the kitchen carrying his shotgun

Opal gasped. "Daddy has a gun?"

Ruby's mouth dropped.

Maggie remained silent as tears found their way down her cheeks again.

Sue laid her hand on Daddy's cheek. "Please be careful."

"I will." Daddy stepped out the door.

Just when Sue had scooped Maggie into her arms, Maggie

never knew, but she was in one of the best places she had ever been. The clock ticked. The rocking chair groaned. Opal and Ruby sat in silence, and everyone strained their ears for the slightest sound. Nothing. That was good. It meant no shouts and no gunshots.

Steps. "What is that?" Opal sat rigid.

"I believe it is your daddy," Sue smiled.

Daddy stepped in the door and shook his head. "Nothing. No shovel. No nothing."

Maggie sat up. "No shovel?"

Daddy shook his head.

"Daddy, he threw a shovel at me!"

Everyone was quiet. Daddy lowered his gaze. "I'll tell you what, Maggie. We'll look in the morning. Maybe we'll find something then. For right now, let's go to bed."

Opal stood. "It was probably just an old dream."

"Dream? A nightmare!" Ruby slipped over to Maggie and grabbed her hand. "You can sleep between us tonight."

Maggie swallowed. "Thanks, Ruby, but I'll be fine." Maggie's eyes slowly traveled to each person in the room. She could see the doubt kindled in their eyes. "It was not a dream or a nightmare. I saw a real man and a real shovel!"

CHAPTER 2

One Hundred Dollars!

Maggie stretched. Fingers of sunshine wavered through the window and danced on the quilt. The warmth sank deep into Maggie and made her feel lazy. She would lie here for just a bit. After all, it was Saturday, her day off. The aroma of breakfast gave life to her tummy, making it rumble and growl.

"Sue, I looked. I didn't find a thing."

Maggie hushed her tummy and listened. She knew she shouldn't. How many times had she gotten in trouble for that very thing? How many times had she gotten by with it? Maggie decided to pretend to be asleep for just a while longer, at least until she heard what Daddy and Sue were talking about in the kitchen.

"Sam, Maggie is not one to make up stories," Sue soothed.

"I'm not saying she made it up. Maybe she just had a very realistic dream."

"I don't know, Sam." Sue paused. "I don't even think she was that scared when she got shut in Mrs. Crenshaw's cellar."

"Mrs. Crenshaw. Some day that woman will meet her maker." Maggie could hear the anger building in Daddy's voice. "I cannot believe Maggie still wants to work for that woman …"

Suddenly, Daddy paused. "Sue, you know it did look as though there might have been a little digging done behind the cow shed."

"Really?"

Daddy sighed. "I couldn't say it was a man with a shovel. A 'coon or some other animal could have done it just as easily. Besides, why would anyone dig behind your cow shed?"

"Mmmm. No earthly reason I know of, but I don't believe Maggie would make up a story," Sue repeated.

"You're right. I'll keep an eye out, at least until Friday."

Maggie could hear Daddy sipping coffee.

"You are still going to go back to the salt mines Friday?"

"They'll give me a job in a flash. I'm sure not getting one here."

"But it is so far away, not to mention dangerous. We almost lost you the last time." Maggie heard Sue's voice quiver.

Daddy groaned. "Sue, you don't think Maggie is making this up so I won't go, do you?"

Opal jabbed Maggie, "You're eavesdropping, aren't you?"

"That'll get you into T-R-O-B-L-E!" Ruby warned.

"That isn't the way you spell trouble." Opal giggled.

Ruby stuck her tongue out at Opal.

"Shhhh!" Maggie held her finger to her lips. She just had to hear.

"I know she doesn't want you to go," Sue spoke.

"Maggie, did you make up the shovel man so Daddy wouldn't go back to the salt mines?" Ruby asked.

"Wow! You had a good idea." Opal sighed in wonder.

"You're sure smart, Maggie," Ruby added.

Maggie had had enough. "No, I did not make it up." She bounded out of bed, went to the doorway and threw back the quilt. "I did not make up the man and the shovel!"

Opal and Ruby crowded behind her.

Daddy and Sue turned toward Maggie. Sue's eyes were wide with surprise.

Daddy set his cup down and swallowed.

Maggie stood with her hands on her hips. "I saw a man out in the dark with a shovel. I thought he was you, but when I called to him, he turned and threw the shovel at me!" She poked herself in the chest to emphasize the man's aim.

"Maggie, what did he look like?" Daddy asked.

Maggie shrugged her shoulders. "He was in the shadows, and after he threw the shovel, I didn't stick around to see what he looked like. I ran to the house!"

"Come here, Maggie." Daddy pushed his chair away from the table and patted his knee. Slowly Maggie crossed to Daddy. He pulled her onto his lap and gently tipped her chin so he could see into her eyes. "Maggie, are you sure you didn't make up this story so I wouldn't leave on Friday?"

Maggie shook her head. "Honest."

"Cross your heart?"

"And hope to die."

"Sam, someone is coming," Sue interrupted. She crossed to the window and lifted the curtain. Opal and Ruby flew to the door, pulled it open and ran across the porch.

"Sam, it's Thomas Gatlin's Hudson," Sue let the curtain fall.

"*The* Thomas Gatlin? This is quite an honor." Daddy swirled the bit of coffee left in his cup. "I wonder what he wants."

Maggie could tell Daddy didn't really think this was an honor. She started to slide from his lap, but Daddy held her close.

Maggie watched through the door the girls had left open. The blue Hudson stopped in a cloud of dust. The car door slammed. Mr. Thomas Gatlin stepped away from the dust cloud and brushed his black suit. "It's not Sunday, and he's got a suit on!" Opal whistled.

"He's got an inside job, Opal," Daddy stated.

Maggie felt Daddy's arm tense up. Daddy didn't even own a suit, at least not one that fit very well. Maggie remembered her mama and daddy's wedding picture. Daddy hadn't looked very comfortable in a suit. Maybe Daddy didn't think much of inside jobs where you had to wear a suit, or maybe he didn't think much of Mr. Thomas Gatlin.

Mr. Gatlin walked to the boxcar. Opal pushed the screen door open for him.

"Morning, ladies."

Both "ladies" giggled.

"Come on in, Mr. Gatlin." Sue stepped to the door.

Mr. Gatlin swept his hat from his head and gazed at Sue. Maggie thought he looked at her for a very long time.

Sue waved toward the table. "Won't you have a seat? We're just about to have breakfast. You're welcome to join us."

Mr. Thomas Gatlin pulled his eyes away from Sue and looked toward the table. "Thanks, but I have already eaten."

Daddy tipped his head. "Thomas."

"Sam," Mr. Gatlin returned.

"Excuse me for not getting up. My lap is full." Daddy patted Maggie's leg and smiled. "Have a seat, Thomas."

Maggie could feel the tension in the room. Opal and Ruby stood in the doorway.

"Mr. Gatlin, would you like a cup of coffee?" Sue asked.

"That would be nice, Sue," Mr. Gatlin said without looking at her. His eyes were on Daddy, and Daddy's eyes were on him. Maggie thought they were sizing up each other.

"What brings you to our place?" Daddy asked.

"Business."

Maggie drew in her breath. Maybe he would offer her daddy a job! That would be a miracle, but the God in her heart was a God of miracles!

"Well, state your business," Daddy told him.

Mr. Gatlin lifted his chin. "My business is with Sue."

Sue stepped around the table to stand behind Daddy. She put her hand on his shoulder before she spoke. "Sam and I are together in all our business. If you have business with me, you have business with Sam."

Mr. Gatlin looked at both of them, set his cup down and leaned back in his chair. "Sue, your ... husband doesn't have a job. Furthermore, he is not going to find a job here in Dodge City. I've talked to all the businesses up and down Main Street in your interest, and I've found there just are no jobs available."

Maggie could feel her cheeks turning red. "Sure there are no jobs for my daddy! That's because you threatened all the people so they wouldn't hire him!"

"Maggie, hush," Daddy warned.

"Hard times." Mr. Gatlin spread his hands.

"Made harder by you," Maggie whispered, but everyone heard it.

"Maggie, no more." Daddy's voice was like ice.

Mr. Gatlin smiled, but Maggie thought his smile didn't reach his heart. "Whatever the cause of the hard times—no rain, no crops, this depression, Hoover, whatever the cause—the times are hard for us all. I just want to make them a little easier for Sue ... and the rest of you."

"And just how are you going to do that?" Daddy asked.

"A job?" Maggie whispered.

"No. No job. Along with the rest of the good people in Dodge City, I have no job to give." Mr. Gatlin chuckled. "It is only because of Sue that I am going to make this offer."

Silence settled in the room. Mr. Gatlin put his hands behind his head. Maggie watched his gold chain swing as it dangled from his vest pocket to the buttonhole.

"I'll buy this dried up pasture and this ... this ... thing you call a house. I'll buy it all for one hundred dollars." Mr. Gatlin swept his arms in a circle around the room.

"A hundred dollars!" Opal gasped.

"Wow!" Ruby echoed.

Sue was silent.

"One hundred dollars?" Daddy asked quietly.

"That's my offer; take it or leave it."

Daddy licked his lips. "Thomas, Sue's 'dried up pasture' is a whole section of land. It is worth much more than one hundred dollars."

Mr. Gatlin leaned his elbows on the table. "If you can find a buyer, it could be worth more. If you can't, it is only worth what you can get for it."

Daddy's eyes pierced Thomas Gatlin's eyes. Finally he spoke, "I take that to mean you have also talked to the good people of Dodge City, and they are not in the market to buy Sue's 'dried up pasture' either."

With a hint of a smile, Mr. Gatlin clasped his hands together. "You may take it however you'd like. One hundred dollars is a lot of money. It could get you out of here and settled some place where you could find a job. It's a good offer."

"We'll leave it." Daddy never took his eyes off Mr. Gatlin.

"Think on it, man. This could buy a clean start for your family."

"No."

"It's a good deal. It's the best deal you are going to get." Mr. Gatlin spread his hands on the table.

Daddy's voice was low, but it echoed in everyone's ears. "I'd sooner make a deal with the devil."

Mr. Gatlin smiled. It made Maggie so cold she thought he might have borrowed his smile from the devil.

Mr. Gatlin slid his chair back and stood. He looked at the floor for a minute, and then leveled his gaze on Daddy. "I'm a generous man. I'll tell you what I'll do. I'll leave the deal open for one week. Maybe you can talk it over. Maybe you will change your mind."

"No need to leave it open, Thomas. There will be no deal. We won't change our minds." Daddy set Maggie down and stood.

Mr. Gatlin flipped his hat against the side of his leg a couple of times and turned toward the door. "If you should change your mind, come by and see me at the bank." When no one answered, Mr. Gatlin slipped his hat on his head. "I'll let myself out." Mr. Gatlin walked to the door, opened it and left. Maggie heard the blue Hudson rev up, spin a circle and grind down the dirt road.

Maggie didn't breathe until the dust settled. She was afraid to say anything, but she wanted to hear what Sue and Daddy would say.

"What do you think that was about?" Sue asked.

Daddy shook his head. "I don't know, but it can't be good."

"Sam, we could sell my land," quietly Sue spoke.

"No. We agreed that selling your land would be the very last thing we would consider. Besides, I would never sell to him."

"Be careful of your pride, Sam."

Daddy looked at Sue. "I won't sell to him, and that is final."

Sue laid her hand on his arm. "Then maybe we could sell to someone else."

Daddy stood. "To whom? From what Mr. Thomas Gatlin told us, I don't think anyone would buy your land, just as no one will hire me."

"We could try. It might be nice to have a clean start. We could go to a place where no one knows us, or maybe even to Hutchinson where everyone thinks of you as a hero!"

"I'd feel as if we were running away. I don't think God honors that, Sue." Daddy pulled his hand over his face. "One hundred dollars sounds like a lot of money, but it isn't. It isn't a lot if you are going against the things you believe in. I believe it would be wrong to make any kind of bargain with Thomas Gatlin. There is a verse in the Bible that says we are not to be unequally yoked together with unbelievers. Thomas Gatlin may go to church every Sunday, but he is just putting in an appearance. If God lives in him, it is not the same God who lives in me."

"It just seems Thomas Gatlin has blocked every road we might take!" Sue waved her hand through the air.

"Yes, it does, but maybe God is using Thomas Gatlin to block those roads. Thomas Gatlin does seem to hate us without a cause." Daddy paused in deep thought. "Maybe we should be trying to find out why he wants to be rid of us. Then maybe things will make sense. Until then, I will not bargain with the man." Daddy seemed to be watching the empty road.

Sue lowered her head. "Sam, I know you are right, and I'll stand behind any decision you make."

Daddy turned to face Sue. "You are a good woman, Sue, a true lady. Thank you."

Then Maggie watched as Daddy wrapped his arms around Sue. His gesture tugged at Maggie's heart, but it didn't rip it open the way it used to.

Gatlin Credit

"The heart of man is deceitfully wicked." Pastor Olson leaned on the pulpit and seemed to examine his congregation.

Maggie looked up at Daddy. She didn't think he was deceitfully wicked. He was honest, kind and hard working … when he could find a job. Just what did Pastor Olson mean by that? Maggie's eyes strayed around the old church. They landed on Mr. Thomas Gatlin. Maggie blinked. He had a grey suit on today. She wondered just how many suits he had. Now *his* heart might be deceitfully wicked. Daddy sure didn't like him. Maybe Pastor Olson was talking to him. Maggie tipped her head. Mr. Thomas Gatlin looked like a nice man. Could Daddy be wrong about him? No. Mr. Thomas Gatlin had talked to all of Dodge City so no one would give Daddy a chance at a job. Maggie frowned. Why had he done that? Opal and Ruby thought it was because he had asked Sue to marry him, and Sue had chosen Daddy instead. A cold shiver ran up Maggie's back. She was so glad Sue had picked Daddy. She liked Sue. Maggie thought about what Sue had given up to marry Daddy. She could have been the richest lady in town.

She could have been living in that mansion across the pasture. Why, Opal and Ruby wouldn't have to share a bed with Maggie. They would have their own beds. They would have their own bedrooms. Sue had picked Daddy. What a miracle. Sue had chosen to stay in her dinky boxcar with Daddy and Maggie rather than to have the riches Mr. Thomas Gatlin could have given her.

"If a man gives his heart to God, God will take his deceitfully wicked heart and make it over anew." Pastor Olson squeezed his left hand with his right hand as if it were a heart.

Maggie looked at Daddy again. That's why Daddy wasn't deceitfully wicked. God lived in his heart. She swung her gaze to Mr. Thomas Gatlin again and squinted. She couldn't see his heart by looking at him, but she sure doubted if God lived there.

"And ye shall know them by their fruit. God tells us we can know a Christian. Their fruit, which is what they produce, will reveal whether they are of the Spirit or not. The fruit of the Spirit will have these qualities: love, joy, peace, longsuffering, gentleness, goodness, faith, meekness and temperance. God's word tells us there is no law against any of these qualities. A person with these fruits will not be breaking any laws. In fact, with these fruits they will draw people to the Lord Jesus Christ." Pastor Olson spread his hands.

Maggie tingled inside. She didn't know what all of those things were, like meekness and temperance, but she thought of Sue. Sue had that kind of fruit, and she had shown Maggie how to get the God up in heaven to be the God in her heart. Mrs. Valina had taught her the way to show God's love to someone like Mrs. Crenshaw, even when she thought Mrs. Crenshaw hated her. Daddy had taught Maggie to be honest and to do what she said she would do.

Maggie peeked over at Mrs. Crenshaw in time to see her twist Cecil's ear and thump Elbert's head while she sat there with a smile, nodding in agreement with everything Pastor Olson preached. Mrs. Crenshaw had never shown Maggie any love or joy. Maggie thought Mrs. Crenshaw was one of the unhappiest people she had ever met. Maggie started marking with her fingers the fruit Pastor Olson named. Did Mrs. Crenshaw have love? No. Joy? No. Peace? Definitely not. Long-suffering? Maggie didn't know what that one meant. Maybe Mrs. Crenshaw had longsuffering because she sure was good at making Maggie suffer! Gentleness? No. Goodness? No. Faith? Mrs. Crenshaw said she had faith, but Maggie didn't know for sure. Meekness and temperance? She would have to ask Sue or Mrs. Valina what these meant. So far, Mrs. Crenshaw hadn't scored very well on Maggie's fruit test.

"Remember, ye shall know them by their works. You are fruit inspectors. You need to be a witness to those who don't bear fruit. By the same token, remember your fruit is being inspected, too." Pastor Olson paused as he searched the congregation. "All of us need to be ready for inspection! Shall we pray?"

Maggie bowed her head. She felt like she was being inspected all right. She'd better find out what those fruits were that she didn't understand, so she would know how to have them.

As Pastor Olson said "Amen," Mr. Thomas Gatlin stood. "Might I have a word with these fine people, Larry?"

Pastor Olson seemed hesitant, but he nodded.

Mr. Gatlin walked up to the front and stood behind the pulpit. Maggie watched Daddy's hand tighten on the arm of the pew.

"Good people of Dodge City, as you well know, Sam Daniels is fairly new to our town. He is an outsider and things have been difficult for him. He couldn't make it on his farm. Sue doesn't have a job, and Sam hasn't been able to find a job. Their sole source of income is what his little waif of a girl can bring home. He is in dire need of some financial help. I have offered to buy Sue's pasture in order to help them relocate, and I've given them some time to accept the offer. Until they accept, I am asking you fine people of Dodge City to extend credit to them. Charge it to my account. I will be glad to take care of this for them." Mr. Gatlin smiled to everyone, but the smile didn't quite make it to his eyes, which he planted on Daddy.

A murmur of awe surged through the crowd.

Daddy's knuckles were white. Slowly he stood. "Mr. Gatlin, that won't be necessary."

"Oh, did you decide to take my offer, Mr. Daniels?" Mr. Gatlin smoothed his hands down the front of his vest.

"No."

"Mr. Daniels, I am just trying to be neighborly and help someone in need." Mr. Gatlin smiled.

"Mr. Gatlin, I would not accept help from you if you were the last man on earth." Daddy turned to leave.

"Pride! Pride goeth before a fall!" Maggie didn't even have to look to see where the voice came from. She would know it anywhere. That voice belonged to Mrs. Crenshaw.

"Mr. Daniels, I may not be the last man on earth, but I assure you, I am the last man in Dodge City." Smugly Mr. Gatlin leaned over the pulpit and squinted at Daddy.

For a long moment, Daddy looked at Mr. Gatlin. He turned. "Sue, girls, let's go home."

Maggie grabbed Opal's and Ruby's hands. As she followed Daddy and Sue down the aisle, she could feel eyes burning into her back. Daddy didn't say a word as he helped Sue into the wagon. Maggie tumbled over the side of the wagon and helped Opal and Ruby in.

"Sam, why do you think he did that?" Sue asked.

"I know why he did that," Daddy said angrily. "He did it so everyone in Dodge City will think he is a good man. If they think he is a good man, they will continue to listen to him and do what he tells them to do."

"Maybe," Sue didn't sound convinced.

"Just think what would happen, Sue, if we started putting things on Mr. Thomas Gatlin's credit. He would let it go until it reached an enormous amount, and then he would come to collect. We wouldn't have the money to pay him, so he would get your 'dried up pasture.' Sue, there would be nothing we could do."

"Sam, you're right." Sue put her hand to her throat. "Why does he want the pasture?"

"Sue, he doesn't. He wanted you. You are a beautiful, delightful Christian woman. You turned him down. I think he just can't bear to look at us. He hates me because I have you. Mr. Gatlin is used to having his way." Daddy shook his head. "He is just having a big temper tantrum the way a little child would do."

Maggie's head swam. Grown-ups weren't always grown up. Everything would be easier if they were. She looked back at the church. Mr. Thomas Gatlin stood on the steps surrounded by people. Maggie decided Mr. Gatlin's fruit wasn't very good. Pastor Olson stood thoughtfully to one side and Maggie wondered if he thought that, too.

Opal slammed her fist into the side of the wagon. "I guess this means we aren't going to take Mr. Gatlin's credit."

"That's exactly what it means, Opal," Maggie told her.

"Dad gum it! I wanted to get some lace gloves."

"Opal. You're not s'posed to say 'dad gum it.'" Ruby shook her finger at Opal. "Mama says ladies don't use glorified curse words."

"Well, I wanted those lace gloves." Opal whined.

"Why? You're not much of a lady. You'd just rip them up," Ruby told her.

"I'm more of a lady than you." Opal shoved her face close to Ruby.

"'Cause you're older? Being older don't make you a lady, and saying 'dad gum it' proves you are not a lady." Ruby glared at Opal.

Opal stuck out her tongue. Ruby grabbed it and pulled.

"EEEOW!"

Both girls began to throw punches.

Maggie took each one's arm and pulled the two girls apart. "Neither one of you will end up being a lady if you act that way."

"But I wanted lace gloves." Opal pouted.

"Gloves won't make you a lady, Opal." Maggie shook her head.

BEEP! BEEP! Mr. Gatlin's Hudson swerved around the wagon. He tipped his hat and waved. The horses reared and bolted up the street. Opal tumbled into Ruby and knocked her flying. Ruby screamed and Maggie grabbed her foot to keep her from bouncing out the back of the wagon. A sharp pain shot through Maggie's chin as she hit something under the straw on the floor of the wagon. Sue hung onto the seat and Daddy hollered "Whoa!" at the horses. At the edge of town the trembling horses stopped. Daddy flipped the reins to Sue and jumped down to check on his horses. Quietly he spoke to them and patted their necks. Opal and Ruby were crying. Maggie was trembling.

"Girls, are you all right?"

Maggie crawled over to Opal and Ruby and put her arms around them. "It's okay. It's okay," she repeated over and over.

Ruby looked at Maggie and gasped. "Maggie! You're bleeding!"

"Maggie?" Sue turned in the seat.

"Maggie." Daddy grabbed the side of the wagon and jumped in. Daddy cradled her face in his hands. "Maggie, Maggie, you're hurt! Let me see."

Maggie reached up to her chin. Just beneath, she felt warm, wet blood. She knew her chin hurt, but she didn't know it was bleeding.

Daddy pulled out his handkerchief and dabbed at the wound. "You've got a pretty good cut. It looks deep."

"Does she need stitches, Sam?" Sue asked.

"And use Mr. Thomas Gatlin's credit?" Daddy shook his head.

"Dr. Nelson isn't that way, Sam." Sue brushed her hair away from her face.

Daddy sighed. "The problem is even good people can be affected by Gatlin's offer."

"Sam, please," Sue pleaded.

Daddy shook his head. "It's okay, Sue, I don't think Maggie needs stitches."

"What are stitches?" asked Ruby.

"It's when the doctor takes a needle and some thread and sews up a hole in your skin! That's what stitches are!" Opal told her.

Ruby wildly grabbed Maggie. "I won't let them do that to you, Maggie!"

"Opal," Sue warned.

Daddy chuckled. "Really, I think she'll be fine without stitches."

"Me, too." Maggie breathed.

"It might leave a scar," Daddy paused.

"Daddy, if it does, it's okay because it's under my chin. No one will ever see it," Maggie pleaded. She only saw a big needle with thread going in white and coming out red.

"If you are sure, Maggie?" Daddy asked.

Maggie nodded. "I'm sure."

"Okay. Keep the handkerchief held tight on your chin, and we'll wash it up when we get home." Daddy tipped his head to one side. "What did you hit anyway?"

Maggie shrugged and pointed. "It was something hard and sharp over there under the hay."

Daddy reached beneath the hay and pulled out a red handled shovel with two blue stripes wrapped around the top of the handle.

"Your shovel, Sam. Oh, Maggie, God was so good to us. You could have been hurt much worse." Sue clasped her arms about her stomach.

"Could she have been killed?" Opal wanted to know.

Sue and Daddy both nodded.

"Oh, Maggie!" Ruby held her tight.

Daddy studied the shovel. He ran his hand through his hair then looked at Sue. "This is not my shovel."

Maggie's heart skipped a beat. She didn't know who owned the shovel, but she had a gut feeling it was the same shovel someone had thrown at her in the night!

CHAPTER 4

Under the Blanket

The crisp, brown grass crunched beneath Maggie's shoes. Dust swirled and made its own little storm with each step. Maggie was late today. Everything was late today.

In the middle of the night, the howling wind had haunted any dreams Maggie might have had. Dust had seeped through tiny cracks not covered, and the old boxcar had a lot of them. Sue had hung wet towels and sheets over all the windows and the door. She had tucked the girls in with a prayer, telling them this was really the best time for a dust storm to hit. "If you sleep through the night," she had said, "the storm will pass faster." Maggie had figured "if" was the secret word in "if you sleep." The wind had whined and made an eerie sound. Opal and Ruby had wanted to snuggle close, but that had made them argue. Maggie had giggled. The wet sheet hanging over the window had seemed to breathe with the wind. If Maggie had been alone, it would have been scary, but with Opal and Ruby, it had been fun. She had told them the wind had awakened the ghosts of the dead. That had stopped the arguing all right, but it had started the scary stories and the trembling. Finally, the two girls had gone to sleep with the blanket pulled over their heads. Then Maggie had lain awake for a long time wishing she hadn't thought about ghosts. She had known the moans and groans were made by the storm, but to Maggie those sounds sure had seemed to come from the souls of the dead.

Valina swung open the back gate. "I knew you'd be late, missy Maggie, so I thought I'd catch you when I saw you coming. We had some storm last night, didn't we?"

"We sure did. That horrible storm started in the afternoon and just kept getting worse. It lasted almost all night! Mama said storms are better in the night than in the day because you can sleep through them, and they seem to end faster. I think I like them during the day better. That wind scares me to death." Maggie shivered.

"Now, missy Maggie, you know the Lord is with you especially during the storms." Valina put her arm about Maggie's shoulders.

"Yes, ma'am, I know it, but I could hear the wind louder than I could hear the Lord."

Valina laughed. "The night wind has a lost moan to it that feels like someone searching the dark. I'll agree with you on that."

"You think so, too?"

"Why shouldn't I, child?" Valina asked.

"You're a grown-up."

Valina's rich laughter comforted Maggie. "Missy, the difference in a grown-up and a child isn't what they feel; it's what they do with what they feel."

"What?" Maggie surely didn't understand that.

"Well, last night during that awful moaning wind I'll be thinking you young ladies tucked your heads under the covers."

"How did you know that?" Maggie was amazed.

"Because that's what I did when I was a child. You see, I wasn't any different than you." Valina chuckled.

"What did you do last night? Did you put your head under the covers?"

"No. I put my head under a different blanket. It is the best blanket ever. It is the blood of Jesus Christ. Then I went to sleep. A Bible verse tells me I can do that. It is Psalms 4:8, 'I will both lay me down in peace, and sleep: for thou, Lord, only makest me dwell in safety.' I knew He would take care of me. After all, He's done it before." Valina smiled.

"Wow! What a blanket. Psalms 4:8?" Maggie asked.

Valina nodded. "It's the best blanket you'll ever find."

"I'm going to memorize that verse, and I'm going to make Opal and Ruby learn it, too."

"That's a good idea. Now you had better take these heaping coals here and be on your way." Valina handed a covered basket to Maggie.

"What is it today?"

"Not much, today." Valina shoved a wisp of curly hair from her forehead. "I had to do a bunch of cleaning before I could get to the cooking. The storm left heaps of dirt and dust. I only had time to throw together some pie dough cookies."

"Pie dough cookies!" Maggie snatched back the cloth and grabbed one. "These are my favorite. I didn't even think you'd have any heaping coals today. Cecil and Elbert can hardly wait for me to get there, and I know Mrs. Crenshaw likes the heaping coals even though she tries her hardest not to let on."

Valina laughed and shoved Maggie on her way. "The good Lord said heaping coals on your enemy would work."

"Mrs. Crenshaw is a for sure enemy, but it is nudging her a tiny bit."

"All in God's time, missy; all in God's time." Valina pushed Maggie on her way.

Maggie walked to the gate and swung it open, stepped through, and then turned to click it shut. She stepped out of her world and into Mrs. Crenshaw's world. Maggie closed her eyes and prayed. "Lord, please be with me today." Maggie felt the warm sunshine on her face and smiled. It was a good day. She felt the God of heaven with her. She crossed the street and started down the tree-lined lane.

"Hold it!" a husky voice ordered as someone shoved a cold metal barrel into the middle of Maggie's back.

Maggie stopped in her tracks.

"Set the basket on the ground and step away," the voice barked.

Maggie set the basket down, stepped back and put her hands on her hips. "Elbert, I know that is you." Maggie laughed.

"Phooey!" Elbert sauntered around to face Maggie. His reddish-brown hair sprawled all over the top of his head. A dirty handkerchief smashed his nose to make a bandana. Only his green eyes danced above it. He twirled the carved stick he used for a gun and dropped it.

Maggie giggled.

"How'd you know it was me?"

"Elbert, I'd know you anywhere." Maggie laughed.

Elbert sighed. "It didn't work, Cecil."

When Secrets *come* Home

Cecil dropped out of the tree beside Maggie. "I told you it wouldn't work."

"It was your idea!" Elbert wailed.

"Not the way you did it." Cecil spread his hands. "You were supposed to wait until I dropped out of the tree on top of her and covered her head with this." He held out a pillowslip. "Then she wouldn't have known it was us because she wouldn't have been able to see you or hear your squeaky voice."

"You gave me the sign!" yelled Elbert.

"I didn't give you the sign. I lost my grip on the branch and almost fell out of the tree." Cecil glared.

"Then that makes it your fault." Elbert crossed his arms and gave a nod making it final.

"I don't care whose fault it was. You're not getting the goodies until after lunch." Maggie snatched the basket and laughed.

"Please, Maggie?" Elbert begged.

"Just tell us what the goodies are." Cecil licked his lips.

"Pie dough cookies." Maggie made the grand announcement.

Elbert fell to the ground and held his tummy. "Maggie, I'm dying for one!"

Maggie giggled. "Okay, guys, but just one."

Elbert reached for a cookie and stopped. "Maggie, what happened to your chin?"

Maggie rubbed her hand over the gash. It was about an inch long. Daddy had decided it needed stitches, but with the decision came the first roaring of the windstorm. Going for stitches had been out of the question. "I fell on a shovel."

"Ooo! Did it hurt?" Elbert groaned.

"Just how do you think it would feel to fall on a shovel?" Maggie frowned.

"Shovel!" Cecil thumped Elbert's head. "Elbert, we've got to find the shovel or we'll be in big trouble. Remember Aunt Louise told us to get it and uncover the tomato plants in the garden." Cecil slapped his leg.

"You can't find the shovel?" Maggie asked.

Cecil shrugged. "Not yet, but we really haven't looked very hard. We just looked in the barn and the tool shed."

"Isn't that where you keep the shovel?"

"I guess, but it ain't there." Cecil threw his hand in the air.

"How long has it been gone?" Maggie asked.

Cecil shrugged his shoulders. He was tired of talking about a dumb shovel. "How about those cookies?"

"Cookie, not cookies." Maggie corrected and watched them each grab and devour a cookie. She smiled. Elbert seemed much nicer since he had asked Jesus to be in his heart. Cecil still meant trouble for Maggie most of the time. He had learned he could use his little brother to get his way around Maggie sometimes. She knew it, but she didn't care. She liked Elbert. He had changed. Maybe Cecil would, too.

"Maggie, Aunt Louise has been looking for you. She sent us out here to find out when you were coming and then tell her," Elbert told her.

"Yeah, she's mad because you're so late, and she hates all the dirt everywhere. She tried to make us dust, but she threw us out 'cause she said we were just stirring it around." Cecil rolled his eyes.

Maggie took a deep breath. "Thanks. I guess I'd better head to the house. You won't have to tell her I'm coming because I'll be there."

Maggie ran the rest of the way down the lane and stopped. Mr. Thomas Gatlin's blue Hudson sat in front of the house.

That shouldn't be unusual. Mrs. Crenshaw and her sister, cousins to Mr. Thomas Gatlin, had been raised most of their lives in the Gatlin mansion. They had come there to live after their mama died. Still, Maggie had never seen Mr. Gatlin at the Crenshaw house before.

Maggie paused. Usually she knocked before she went into the house. Maggie didn't have to, but she felt better about it when she did. Mrs. Crenshaw was probably busy with her guest today, so Maggie guessed she shouldn't bother her. Maggie would just go on in and start dusting. The boys had pretty much told her dusting would be what she would be doing today. Maggie slipped in and went to the kitchen. She set the basket of cookies on the cabinet and went to get the dust cloth and the furniture oil. Maggie went to the entryway to start. As she dusted, her thoughts wandered. Had it been the Crenshaw shovel in the back of the Daniels' wagon, and who had thrown it at her? Maggie's heart started beating faster. It could not have been one of the boys because it had definitely been a man. Besides, she could not believe either of the boys was brave enough to be outside at night. Maggie felt sick at her stomach. If the shovel belonged to the Crenshaws, and the boys hadn't thrown it, only Mr. Crenshaw could have done it. She liked Mr. Crenshaw and she thought he liked her. Could she be wrong? No. Maggie knew he liked her. But if the shovel did belong to the Crenshaws, why would Mr. Crenshaw be digging behind their cow shed? Maggie grabbed her tummy, leaned against the wall and slid down. In her mind she kept saying, "Please, Lord, don't let it be Mr. Crenshaw."

"Louise, you have got to think harder. Did you ever see Mother or Daddy put papers in some unusual place?"

"Maybe the family Bible." Mrs. Crenshaw suggested.

"No. I've already looked there."

"What papers, Thomas?"

"Nothing important, just keepsakes and such." Mr. Gatlin paused.

Maggie didn't even think about the fact that she was eavesdropping. She was too involved in her own thoughts about the shovel and Mr. Crenshaw. The things she heard seemed distant and far away.

"Think, Louise, think."

"Thomas, maybe you could ask that woman your mama always had helping out at the house. What was her name? It was a weird name … Varnie … Victoria … something starting with V." Mrs. Crenshaw's voice trailed off.

"Valina?" Mr. Gatlin asked.

"That's it!" Mrs. Crenshaw seemed relieved.

Maggie now turned her full attention to the conversation in the other room.

"I really would rather not ask her," Mr. Gatlin sighed. I'd rather keep this in the family."

"Then it must be important, Thomas."

"It's not important to anyone but me. Now think, Louise," Mr. Gatlin ordered.

"Thomas, that was years ago. Right now, I can only think of the dust from that horrible storm. I didn't sleep a wink last night with all the howling wind! I have so much laundry from the wet towels and sheets we had to stretch over the windows and doors. To top it all off, Maggie hasn't shown up yet to help me." Mrs. Crenshaw almost screeched.

"Louise, do you still have Sam Daniels' girl working for you?" Mr. Gatlin quietly asked.

"Well, yes, Thomas. I need the help since I have Selma's boys. I hope that sister of mine gets well pretty soon. I just don't know how much more I can take. I certainly know why my sister is sick. If I had those boys all the time, plus the younger one and a baby on the way, I would be bedfast, too!" Mrs. Crenshaw whined. "I sure hope she hurries and has her baby. It will probably be another boy!"

"Louise." Mr. Gatlin pulled her back to the subject at hand. "I want you to get rid of that girl."

"What?"

"I want you to get rid of that girl. I don't want her working for you anymore."

"But, Thomas, yesterday in church you said you wanted to help Sam Daniels in any way you could. You even said his girl was the only source of income they had, so why would you want me to fire her?" Mrs. Crenshaw asked, puzzled.

"You don't have to fire her. You can get rid of her in many different ways. If you don't want to fire her, make it so hard she will quit," he suggested.

"Thomas, I don't understand you." Mrs. Crenshaw flatly stated.

"Fire the girl!"

"I can't." Mrs. Crenshaw paused. "She doesn't work for me. She works for my husband."

Maggie felt Mr. Gatlin pound his hand against the wall. Quickly she shook her head and pulled herself to her feet. Why did Mr. Thomas Gatlin care if she worked for Mrs. Crenshaw? Maggie stood with the dust cloth in her hand. Mr. Thomas Gatlin stormed out of the room and ran into her. Maggie tumbled and skidded across the wooden floor.

"Watch where you are going!" he barked.

Mrs. Crenshaw had followed him, "Thomas, what is the matter with you?"

Thomas Gatlin pointed at Mrs. Crenshaw. "I mean it. I want it done, and the sooner the better!" He turned and stormed out the door.

When the door slammed, the silence settled in. Slowly Maggie got to her feet. Mrs. Crenshaw seemed to notice her for the first time. "It's about time you got here." She stopped and sucked in her breath. "My goodness. You are bleeding."

Maggie reached up to her chin. It bled, all right. It poured blood. She must have hit it when Mr. Thomas Gatlin sent her flying.

"Quickly, girl! Get to the kitchen and put a cool rag on it before you get blood all over everything!" Mrs. Crenshaw shooed her away.

Maggie gladly went. She just wished she could go home instead of to the kitchen.

CHAPTER 5

Fruit Inspecting

Finally! Maggie didn't know there could be so much dust. She had mopped and dusted from the moment she had stepped into Mrs. Crenshaw's house until the time she stepped out the door. Half of Oklahoma must have blown across Kansas and settled in Mrs. Crenshaw's house. Maggie swiped her arm across her forehead and looked at the dirt on her sleeve. She patted the skirt of her dress and watched as dust puffed out of it. She needed a bath. She picked up her basket of heaping coals and peeked inside. It was empty. All the pie dough cookies were gone. The Crenshaws must have eaten them all at lunch. Maggie was glad she had snatched a cookie before she left Mrs. Valina's house. Maggie's tummy rumbled. She hadn't gotten to eat because she was upstairs mopping at lunchtime. Mrs. Crenshaw had said because she was late in getting to work, she would have to work through lunch. Maggie reached for the doorknob and gasped as the door swung wide.

It was Mr. Crenshaw. Maggie's heart began pounding. All she could think of was the shovel!

"Maggie, are you still here?" Mr. Crenshaw seemed surprised.

Maggie nodded. Partly she was too tired to talk, and partly she was afraid to say anything.

Mr. Crenshaw knelt down. "Maggie, are you okay?"

Again, Maggie nodded.

"Maggie, you have blood dried on your face." Mr. Crenshaw reached out to her.

Maggie swallowed. "I … it's okay."

"Maggie, what happened?"

That was the last thing Maggie wanted to talk about now. Just what could she say? Someone threw a shovel at me in the night. Then they hid it in our wagon, and I fell on it. Mr. Crenshaw, did you throw the shovel at me? Maggie couldn't say a thing. Tears started building.

"Maggie?" Mr. Crenshaw waited.

Mrs. Crenshaw flounced down the stairs. "Oh, you're finally home."

"Louise, Maggie has blood on her face. Do you know what happened?" Mr. Crenshaw asked.

Mrs. Crenshaw waved her hand. "Still? Maggie, I thought I told you to go clean yourself up. I hope you didn't get it on anything important."

"Louise, what happened?" Mr. Crenshaw asked again.

"Well, the girl would stand in the way. Thomas was here. He was not altogether happy when he left, so he came storming around the corner and collided with her. She should have heard him coming and moved out of the way."

"What was Thomas doing here, Louise?" Mr. Crenshaw wanted to know.

Mrs. Crenshaw looked at Maggie. "That is something I will have to talk to you about in private."

Mr. Crenshaw drummed his fingers on the porch floor and stood. "Okay, Louise, we will talk later."

Maggie inched out the door. "I really need to be going,"

Mr. Crenshaw turned to Maggie. "Oh, before you go, Maggie, I want to ask you to wear your Sunday best when you come here tomorrow. I'm taking you to work with me. I think it would be good for you to be acquainted with the banking business. How do you like that?" Mr. Crenshaw beamed.

"Arnold Jack Crenshaw, you cannot mean that!" Mrs. Crenshaw shouted.

"And why not?"

"Because she is just a … a … a nothing! Why, look at her. Do you think people want to see that when they come into the bank?" Maggie thought Mrs. Crenshaw had her neck stuck out like one of her strutting turkeys.

Maggie smiled. No matter how scared she might be of Mr. Crenshaw, Maggie would rather be with him. Besides, anything that would throw Mrs. Crenshaw into a tantrum was worthwhile. "I would be glad to go with you, Mr. Crenshaw," Maggie quietly spoke, and figured she would have to ask God up in heaven to forgive her for it later.

"That," Mrs. Crenshaw pointed to Maggie, "will probably cost you your job, Arnold! Mark my warning."

"Louise, I am the bank president." Mr. Crenshaw tipped his head to the side.

Mrs. Crenshaw glared, and then turned to Maggie. "Young lady, you had better clean up."

"Yes, ma'am." Maggie took a step backward. "I'll go home right now and do that." She turned and ran down the steps and up the tree lined lane.

"See you bright and early tomorrow!" Mr. Crenshaw shouted after her.

Maggie was glad to be out of there. She didn't stop running until she came to the pasture gate. Things had not gone well today at all. She seemed to be stepping out of the frying pan and into the fire. Working with Mrs. Crenshaw was bad enough, but Mr. Crenshaw? Just why did he want her to go to work with him? Had he thrown the shovel? If he had ... Maggie shook her head. It just could not have been him. Maybe the boys had found the Crenshaw shovel today. That would be the first thing she would ask them in the morning, if she saw them before she left for work with Mr. Crenshaw.

Maggie's thoughts took her to Mrs. Valina's back door. "Mrs. Valina?" she called.

Maggie watched through the screen door as Mrs. Valina's slow sway brought her across the kitchen. "Come on in, child."

Maggie pulled the door open and stepped in.

"Lord have mercy. What happened to you?" Valina grabbed Maggie's arm and pulled her into the light of the window. "Where there isn't dirt there is blood." Without waiting for an answer, Valina dipped a clean cloth in water and began gently sponging Maggie's face. Maggie didn't say a word. When Valina finished, she sat back and surveyed her work. "Hmmm ... I guess it looked worse than it was, but this here gash, now, it looks to me as if it should have had stitches. Just what did that?"

"A shovel."

"You use the wrong end of the shovel?" Valina smiled as she led Maggie to a chair, and then sat down across the table from her. "Now, tell me all about it."

Maggie stretched her arms out on the table and clasped her hands. "Mrs. Valina, Friday night when everyone was asleep except me, I heard this clanking noise outside. I looked out the window, but I couldn't see anything. I kept hearing it though, so I slipped outside to see if I could find out what it was, and I saw a man digging behind our cow shed. I thought it was my daddy, so I called to him. He turned around and threw his shovel at me!"

"He hit your chin with a shovel?" Valina's eyes were huge. "Lord have mercy."

Maggie shook her head. "No. He missed me by this much." Maggie held her fingers apart and pinched the air. "I felt it whiz by my head. I ran to the house and jumped in bed with Mama and Daddy. I told them what had happened. Daddy went out to look. He didn't find anything, and mostly he didn't find the shovel someone threw at me. Mrs. Valina, it was gone. Worst of all, Daddy didn't believe me. He thought I made it up."

"Why would he think that, child?" Valina asked.

"He thought I did it so he wouldn't go back to the salt mines in Hutchinson."

Quietly Valina asked, "Did you make it up?"

Maggie shook her head.

Valina squinted. "How did you get that cut? You did tell me it came from a shovel."

"A shovel cut me, but it didn't happen until after church on Sunday. Mr. Thomas Gatlin drove by our wagon and tooted his horn. It scared our horses, and they took out running. Ruby almost flew out of the wagon, so I grabbed her foot to keep her inside. Only my chin landed on the shovel hidden under the straw in the wagon."

"Mmmm, mmmm." Valina shook her head. "That's bad."

Maggie shrugged. "It hurt, but in a way it was good. Daddy dug out the shovel from the straw and found out it wasn't his. Then he started believing me."

"Did your daddy know whose shovel it is?"

Maggie bit her bottom lip. "No, but I might."

"Well, child, whose shovel is it?" Valina spoke quietly.

Maggie raised her eyes to look into Mrs. Valina's. She rubbed her hand over her face. "Mrs. Valina, I think it might belong to the Crenshaws."

Valina jumped up. "That woman. Lord have mercy on her soul. If she be trying to hurt you, so help me I'll …"

Maggie interrupted, "No, she didn't do it. It was a man."

Valina's mouth fell open as she realized who it must have been. She sank back down in her chair. "Mr. Crenshaw?" she whispered.

Maggie nodded.

"Oh, missy Maggie, it couldn't have been Mr. Crenshaw. Why, he worships the ground you walk on." Valina stretched her hand across the table to pat Maggie's. "Why would you think that?"

"When I got there this morning Cecil said he couldn't find their shovel. He had looked in the barn and the tool shed, and he hadn't found it."

Valina blinked. "It seems to me it just means Cecil hadn't found the shovel yet. You know Cecil. He doesn't spend a whole lot of time looking for something that will make him have to work. Why, I'll be willing to bet if you go to the shed first thing in the morning and scrounge around a bit, you'll find that shovel."

"I'm not working there tomorrow. I'm going to work at the bank with Mr. Crenshaw." Maggie paused. *"Mrs. Valina, do you think Mr. Crenshaw wants to get me alone to kill me?"*

Valina chuckled. "You been reading scary books."

"You don't think he wants to kill me?" Hope filled Maggie.

Valina shook her head. "Mr. Crenshaw is the best of the lot. He dotes on you, child. Anyone with eyes in their head can see that. No, ma'am, I don't think you have a worry in the world where it concerns Mr. Crenshaw, but I'll tell you what you need to do. Did you listen to Pastor Olson's sermon on Sunday?"

Maggie nodded.

"Good. Missy, you become a fruit inspector. You think on everything Mr. Crenshaw has done concerning you. Then you weigh it out. Is it good fruit, or is it bad fruit? When you're done, you can decide whether he threw that shovel or not."

Maggie blinked. "Thanks, Mrs. Valina. You always have the best answers and know exactly what to do."

Valina laughed. "I sure wish I always knew what to do." She stood. "Well, child, you had best be on your way home, and don't forget to take a bath. After all, tomorrow you'll be a banker."

Maggie giggled as she went out the door. What would she do without Mrs. Valina? She helped her every time. Mrs. Valina must be the wisest person Maggie knew.

The grass was as dry and crunchy as it had been in the morning. Maggie looked up to the sky. "Dear God up in heaven, please send us some rain!"

There wasn't even a cloud in the sky, but God probably wouldn't have to use clouds to bring rain if He didn't want to. Maggie laughed. That would be funny. She started thinking about Mr. Crenshaw and fruit inspecting. Mr. Crenshaw had hired her. Mr. Crenshaw had overpaid her, and he had given her tips when Mrs. Crenshaw had taken away money from her wages. Mr. Crenshaw had stood up for her against Mrs. Crenshaw. Mr. Crenshaw had walked her to the gate just to visit with her. Those were just some of the good things Mr. Crenshaw had done. Maggie tried to think of some bad things. The only thing that came close was the shovel incident, and she couldn't be sure he had done that. In fact, now that she had examined his fruit, she didn't see any way he could have done it. Maggie smiled. She didn't fear Mr. Crenshaw anymore.

With all her fruit inspecting, Maggie had crossed the pasture, and now she stopped on the steps of the porch. She saw three boxes of groceries lined up next to Opal and Ruby, who were itching to dig in.

"No one touches a thing," Daddy ordered. "Is that understood?"

"Yes, sir," Ruby mumbled.

"Why?" Opal asked.

"We did not order these groceries. That's why." Daddy declared, sternly.

"But we need them," Opal reasoned.

"What we don't need is the credit."

"But Mr. Gatlin told the people to put it on his credit." Opal spread her hands and wailed.

"If we take the merchandise, Mr. Thomas Gatlin will keep track of every single charge. When there is a huge amount of charges, he will come and try to collect. When we can't pay, he will take your mama's land," Daddy explained.

"That's not very nice." Ruby tipped her head.

"No, it's not very nice," Daddy agreed.

"But Mr. Gatlin looks like such a nice man." Opal frowned.

"Opal, looks are deceiving," Daddy told her. "I'll hitch up the wagon and take this back. You girls can ride along if you want to."

Maggie just wanted to take a bath.

CHAPTER 6

The Trojan Horse

Maggie had decided not to tell Daddy and Sue about the missing shovel at the Crenshaws. It probably didn't amount to anything. Cecil may have even found it by now. Besides, Daddy was too involved with the three boxes of groceries to worry about a little thing like a shovel. Daddy had hitched the horses, loaded up the groceries and the girls, and headed for town.

Maggie sank into the warm water in the galvanized tub they used for taking baths. Sue had taken one look at her and started heating water.

Maggie's tummy growled.

Sue laughed. "And what kind of monster was that?"

"My tummy!" Maggie giggled.

"Didn't you eat?" Sue asked.

"No. Mrs. Crenshaw said I had to work through lunch because I was late this morning."

"What?" Sue swung around from cooking at the stove and shook the wooden spoon in the air. "Why you continue to work there I'll never know. That woman will have so much to answer for at the pearly gates. I wouldn't even want to be close to her shoes. When your daddy finds out, he probably won't let you go back."

Maggie stopped blowing bubbles and looked at Sue. "You can't tell him."

"Maggie, I don't keep secrets from your daddy," Sue spoke honestly.

Maggie pleaded, "Please, just don't tell him until he finds a job here."

"Oh, Maggie, you don't know what you are asking of me. A husband and wife should never have secrets. Honesty is the best thing for any healthy relationship."

"It wouldn't be dishonest. It would be waiting until the right time. That's important in a relationship, too. Isn't it?" Maggie asked.

Sue laughed. "Maggie, some day you may become a lawyer!" Sue sobered. "Maggie, I'll not make you any promises. I won't keep things from your daddy. You may not understand that now, though there will be a time when I hope you not only understand, but you also choose to make that a rule you live by."

Maggie took a deep breath. In that moment, she decided they didn't need to know about the Crenshaw shovel.

Maggie had barely gotten out of the tub and into her nightgown when Daddy burst through the door with Opal and Ruby following. He stopped in front of Sue. "Do you know where these groceries came from?"

Sue's eyes were wide. "No."

"From Mr. Thomas Gatlin himself!" Daddy slammed his fist into his hand.

"What?"

"Mr. Thomas Gatlin waltzed into Cooper's Mercantile, told them to gather up all the things Mrs. Cooper thought we might need, and then he paid for it." Maggie had never seen her daddy so mad.

Sue put out her hand to calm him. "Sam, settle down. You took it back, so everything will be fine."

"No, Sue, it won't be fine. Mr. Thomas Gatlin took the receipt. They wouldn't take the groceries back without the receipt. Gatlin told them they were not to take anything back." Daddy began pacing in circles around the table.

"I guess we'll have to keep them, then. We don't want to look a gift horse in the mouth," Sue reasoned.

"Gift horse?" Daddy stopped pacing. His eyes were wild. "Trojan horse would be more like it. Sue, you remember the Trojan horse, don't you? It was a gift, too … a gift of death!"

"Sam," Sue tried to reach him.

Daddy shoved his fingers through his black hair. "Sue, there must be thirty dollars of groceries. There is no way we can ever pay that back."

Maggie bit her lip. Thirty dollars was a lot of money. It would take her a long time to make that much.

"Sam, maybe he won't charge us for them." Sue tried to soothe him.

Daddy rubbed his chin. "Sue, you are talking about Mr. Thomas Gatlin. He took the receipt and kept it. Why do you think he kept it?"

"Maybe he threw it away later."

"I don't think we had better plan on it." Daddy sank into Sue's rocker.

A knock on the screen door made everyone jump. Opal ran and opened it. Slowly she led in a lanky boy who Maggie thought to be about fifteen. He smiled and laid a brown paper wrapped package in the middle of the table.

Daddy pulled himself up in the rocker. "What is this?"

"Well, sir," the boy cleared his throat, "it's some yard goods from Mabel's Yard Goods store."

"Why?"

The boy shuffled his feet. "I'm just the delivery boy, sir. I don't ask why. I just deliver things where they tell me to deliver them."

"Do you know who bought them?" Daddy asked.

"Well, sir, I was in the store when Mr. Gatlin come in. He told Mrs. Mabel to pick out some pieces of cloth for the family, some pretty stuff for the women folk and some plain stuff for … I guess you. You'll find a small sack inside the bundle with needles and thread and buttons." The boy stopped and looked at Maggie.

Maggie thought he had probably expected everyone to be happy and excited. Maybe he didn't know what to say next because they weren't.

"Son, is there a receipt?" Daddy asked.

"No, sir. Mr. Gatlin paid for it, so he took the receipt."

Maggie could see Daddy's jaw muscles jumping.

"Son, you'll have to take it back." Daddy was firm.

Panic shot from the boy's eyes. "Please, sir. If I take it back, it will mean my delivery job. Mr. Gatlin as much as told me so." The boy twisted his hands around the hat he held. "And I did hear him tell Mrs. Mabel not to take the yard goods back, either. He seemed pretty proud of himself. He said you folks really needed it, and he was happy he could do something to help. He said he wished he could see the surprised look on your faces."

"I'll bet he did," Daddy almost whispered.

"So, sir, can I leave the bundle?" he asked.

Maggie could tell Daddy didn't like it, but he nodded.

The boy backed to the door and took two giant steps across the porch. Maggie thought he wanted out of there before Daddy could change his mind.

Again Daddy ran his fingers threw his hair. He turned and sat at the table in front of the package and stared at it.

"Can we open it?" Opal whispered.

"Please?" Ruby added.

Daddy looked across to Sue. Maggie thought he looked like someone who must be lost and looking for a way home.

Sue answered, "We could look and maybe figure the cost."

Daddy shrugged, "Might as well."

No one reached for the brown paper package. Finally, Daddy pushed it toward Sue. With shaking fingers, Sue untied the twine holding it together. She pulled the paper away, and saw the little sack with the thread and buttons on top. Beneath it lay a folded piece of lavender cloth with tiny purple flowers. Maggie put her hand over her mouth. It had to be the prettiest material she had ever seen.

Opal couldn't contain herself. She reached beneath the purple and yanked out a piece of yellow polka-dotted material. She hugged it and caressed it. "Yellow! It's my favorite color! It will look so good on me!"

Maggie had to agree. With Opal's dark hair, the yellow was perfect.

Under the yellow was a piece of baby blue and white check-ered. Ruby pulled that piece away to reveal material of pale green strewn with dainty daisies. She didn't say a word, but everyone knew which piece she wanted.

Maggie looked at Daddy. The color had drained from his face. Sue quietly collected and stacked the goods. "Ladies, let's get the table ready for supper. Maggie, go put these things in my bedroom."

Daddy didn't even look up. "How much do you reckon, Sue?"

Sue closed her eyes. "A lot, Sam. A lot."

"But how much?"

"Maybe twenty dollars."

Daddy groaned.

Supper that night was very quiet. Daddy didn't say a word. Maggie knew Opal and Ruby wanted to ask if they could keep the material, because Opal had mouthed to Maggie, "Ask if we can keep it!"

Maggie shook her head, glad Opal seemed to take the hint and not ask herself, or try to get Ruby to ask.

Maggie was sure Sue hadn't dared to use any of the groceries from the boxes. Finally, supper was over and the dishes cleared away. Sue shooed the girls toward their bedroom. "I'll come and tuck you in pretty soon. Go ahead and get in bed."

Opal broke the silence first. "I feel like a princess. I'm going to look like one, too. I'll be a beautiful princess in a yellow dress."

"If Daddy lets you." Maggie pulled the covers back.

"Oh, Maggie." Opal groaned. "Do you really think he will make us take it back?"

"I don't know, but I do know you and Ruby better not bother him about it. If you do, the answer will for sure be 'NO!'"

Opal smashed her lips together in a determined line. "Then I will not say a word about my beautiful material. Ruby, you'd better not either."

Ruby crawled into bed and over to the wall. "I didn't, even when you wanted me to."

"Well, make sure you don't." Opal warned as she snuggled beside Ruby.

Maggie laughed. "Opal, you're the one I'm worried about."

"What do you mean?" Opal rose up on one elbow.

"It means you're a blabbermouth." Ruby giggled.

"I am not." Opal turned toward Ruby.

Sue lifted the quilt the girls used for their door. "Sometimes Opal you tend to talk before you think. We all do." Sue smiled and sat on the edge of their bed.

"Do we get to keep all that beautiful material?" Opal really wanted to know.

Sue laid her hand against Opal's cheek. "I don't know. Your daddy and I will pray about it, and when God gives us an answer, we'll let you know."

"Okay, but I'm going to pray the answer is 'yes!'" Opal told Sue.

Sue laughed. "You do that, Opal. You do that."

Maggie picked at the stitching on their cover. "Mama?"

Sue seemed to glow when Maggie called her Mama. "Yes, Margaret Pearl?"

Maggie smiled. "What did Daddy mean about the gift horse being the Trojan horse?"

Sue took a deep breath. "The Trojan horse was a gift to Troy, an ancient city that seemed to be invincible."

"What is invincible?" Ruby asked.

"Invincible means the enemy could not beat them. It was impossible, no matter what they did, or how strong they were."

Ruby nodded.

"Anyway, the city of Troy had huge thick walls around it with heavy gates the soldiers guarded all the time. The enemy couldn't get close enough to the city because soldiers on the top of the walls would shoot arrows at them, or pour hot oil on them.

"Ow! That would hurt." Ruby pulled her cover tighter under her chin.

"Yes, it would. It sometimes even killed them. Because of those things, the enemy just could not get into the city. Finally, the enemy left, but their leader didn't give up. He thought and thought until he came up with a great idea. He gathered his men and told them if they could not defeat Troy from the outside, they would do it from the inside. All his army thought he was crazy. They laughed at him. They said the problem was they couldn't get inside Troy in the first place. He assured them he had thought of a way to get inside the city. Then they listened to him. They built a giant wooden horse as a gift to the people of Troy. They wheeled it to the gates of Troy and unveiled their gift. Then they left. The people of Troy thought it was a magnificent gift of submission. They waited until the enemy had gone. Then they opened their gates and hauled the huge horse into their city. The people of Troy celebrated royally. They didn't know the Trojan horse was hollow, and it was filled with enemy soldiers.

That night in the quiet the soldiers sneaked out of the horse and conquered the city of Troy."

Maggie's eyes were wide. "So the gift to the city of Troy was really to destroy Troy!"

"Yes, Maggie, it was."

"It wasn't a very nice gift even if it looked magnificent." Maggie understood.

"That's right, Maggie," Sue nodded.

"That's what Daddy meant about Mr. Thomas Gatlin's gifts to us, isn't it, Mama?" Maggie's tummy felt a little sick.

"You mean Mr. Gatlin's gifts are to destroy us?" Opal sat up in bed.

Sue nodded again. "I'm sorry, Opal."

"But they are so beautiful." Opal sank back into bed.

"So was the Trojan horse." Maggie whispered.

CHAPTER 7

Stub Huggins

Streaks of blushing pink layered the morning sky. The sun pulled a dusty blue robe behind her, putting out all the twinkling stars. She would rule over the day like royalty. Maggie twirled. She had on her pink rosebud dress that once belonged to her mama. Sue had fixed it so it would fit her. Maggie wondered if Mrs. Crenshaw would remember it. Maggie remembered what Mrs. Crenshaw had said. "That dress the poor girl had on … why, it must have been three or four sizes too big, besides being as old as the hills!" Just what might Mrs. Crenshaw say today? Maggie stood tall and straightened her wonderful dress. She would walk like a lady and make both of her mamas proud! She looked into the sky. "Please tell Mama 'Hello,'" Maggie whispered, "and please let Mama know I'm being taken care of by a mama named Sue. Thank you."

The day grew brighter. She'd better hurry so Mr. Crenshaw wouldn't have to wait on her. Apprehension and excitement collided, leaving Maggie with a grand turmoil inside. She really did like Mr. Crenshaw, but the missing shovel worried her. The first thing she would do would be to scrounge up Cecil and ask if he had found the shovel.

"There you are, missy!" Valina waved. She stood at the gate with the heaping coals basket looped over her arm. "Don't you look mighty fancy today?" Valina sniffed the air. "And I see you took my advice and soaked in a tub."

Maggie laughed. "What's in the basket?"

"You can't smell it, missy?"

Maggie filled her lungs. "Homemade bread. You must have been up mighty early."

"You know Mr. Gatlin. He needs his bread. He tells me to make him a list and he brings the supplies. He always brings extra so Martin and I can have some of the goodies, too. You know I love to bake, and I love it to be appreciated." Valina's deep laughter filled the morning.

"Appreciate it? Cecil and Elbert even emptied slop buckets for it." Maggie giggled.

"Yes, missy, they sure did, didn't they?" Valina snickered as she gave Maggie a hug and pushed her through the gate. "I'll be asking the good Lord to take care of you today," Valina called as she waved.

"Thanks." Maggie turned and sailed down the lane. She stopped. Mr. Crenshaw had the sedan pulled in front of the house. That seemed strange because he always walked to work. He had said he needed the exercise. Maybe he wanted this day to be special. Maggie guessed she would get to ride to the bank in style. First, though, she had to see Cecil.

Maggie's footsteps sounded hollow on the wooden porch as she crossed it. She listened. It sounded as if they were eating

breakfast. How could she ask Cecil about the shovel with everyone at the table? She had to find out if Cecil had found the shovel before she drove off alone with Mr. Crenshaw. Maggie knocked on the door.

"Bother. Always. Someone knocks just as we sit down to a meal. One of you boys make yourself useful. Go answer the door!" Mrs. Crenshaw ordered.

Maggie crossed her fingers. "Please let it be Cecil."

She listened to the footsteps run across the floor. The screen door screeched open. "What do you want?" Cecil asked.

"Did you find the shovel?" Maggie hissed.

"No. Do you know where it is?"

Maggie felt cold all over. She shook her head.

Cecil wadded his fist and whacked his forehead. "Aunt Louise said if I didn't find it, she'd make me crawl through the garden on my hands and knees, uncovering those plants." Cecil groaned.

"Cecil, is that Maggie?" Mr. Crenshaw called.

"Yes, sir."

"Bring her on in."

Mrs. Crenshaw set the jar of jelly on the table. "Good. Maggie has time enough to do the dishes before she goes off to the bank with you."

Maggie stood in the doorway holding her breath. She didn't want to do dishes in her Sunday best.

Mr. Crenshaw laid his fork down. "Louise, Maggie won't have time to do dishes before we go. Besides, she would ruin her pretty dress."

Mr. Crenshaw winked at Maggie, and she let out her breath.

"Have you eaten, Maggie?" he asked.

"No, sir."

"Pull up a chair." Mr. Crenshaw motioned to an empty chair in the corner.

Mrs. Crenshaw leaned over the table and hissed. "She is hired help! Hired help does not sit at the table."

Cecil and Elbert stopped eating and started watching.

Mr. Crenshaw studied his toast. "Louise, this is my house. I'll say who can sit at my table."

Louise folded her napkin and stood.

"While you are up, Louise, would you please grab a plate for Maggie?" Mr. Crenshaw took a bite of his toast.

Mrs. Crenshaw's mouth dropped open.

Cecil stifled a giggle.

Mrs. Crenshaw turned her glare on the boys. Both boys quickly looked away, and they shoved something into their mouths.

"Uh ... uh ... I ... uh ... know where the plates are, Mr. Crenshaw. I can get it myself," Maggie stuttered, "and I just want a slice of this bread."

"In that basket?" Mr. Crenshaw asked. "Is it like the bread you brought the other day?"

Maggie nodded.

"Wish you had gotten here sooner. That was the best bread I've ever tasted."

Mrs. Crenshaw threw her napkin on the table and stomped out of the kitchen. Maggie wanted to smile, but tomorrow she would have to work under Mrs. Crenshaw again. Tomorrow she would pay dearly for today.

After breakfast, Mr. Crenshaw pushed away from the table. "Are you ready to go to work with me, Maggie?"

Maggie jumped up. "Yes, sir!"

"Head on out to the car while I tell Louise good bye and get my hat," he told her.

Maggie skipped through the house, across the porch, down the steps and to the car. She opened the door to step in and stopped. A pair of dirty work boots sat on the floorboard. She had never seen Mr. Crenshaw wear work boots, and why would they be in the car? Any chores he might do would be done at home. Besides, Daddy had said banking was an easy, sit-down, eight-to-five desk job. Why would Mr. Crenshaw ever need work boots with a job like that? Maggie thought Mrs. Crenshaw would surely make him keep them in the barn. She wouldn't want them in the car.

"Ready?"

Maggie nearly jumped out of her skin.

"Crawl on in, and I'll shut the door."

Maggie crawled in.

Mr. Crenshaw started up the engine and headed down the lane. Maggie felt the vibration and wanted to giggle. At the end of the lane, Mr. Crenshaw turned his car in the opposite direction from the bank. Maggie reached over and tightened her grip on the door. She wanted to ask where they were going, but she didn't know what to say.

"We'll use the Gatlin shortcut," Mr. Crenshaw told her. "I've some bank business with the people who live on the other side of the Gatlin estate."

Maggie's head swung to Mr. Crenshaw. "With my daddy?"

Mr. Crenshaw chuckled. "No. It's with the people on the other side of the Gatlin estate."

At the Gatlin gate, Martin walked into the middle of the road with his shotgun. "This be private property. There's the 'NO TRESPASSING' sign."

"Martin, it's me. I'm family."

Martin walked up to the car window shaking his head. "Orders, Mr. Crenshaw. Mr. Gatlin told me I got to stop everyone."

"Mr. Gatlin is not quite himself lately. I'll tell him you are doing a fine job." Mr. Crenshaw stretched his hand out to shake with Martin.

"I see you got yourself some mighty fine company there. Morning to you, Miss Maggie." Martin tipped his hat.

Maggie smiled and waved.

"We'll be on our way. I've got to make a call at Stub Huggins' place." Mr. Crenshaw revved his engine.

Martin raised his eyebrows and chuckled. "Luck to you."

Maggie wondered what he meant.

Mr. Crenshaw laughed and swung the sedan to the side of the Gatlin out buildings, and then took a right. The auto bounced across the pasture for a couple of miles and stopped at a gate. Mr. Crenshaw jumped out of the car, opened the gate and climbed back in the auto to drive through. He stopped again, got out to close the gate behind them, and returned to the car. "Not far now, Maggie."

Maggie's heart pumped. She loved the wind blowing her hair. She crossed her arms on the window ledge and hung her head out further.

"Here we are." Mr. Crenshaw turned into a drive spotted with a few brown evergreens. Maggie felt sure they must be dead. As they drove closer, Maggie thought the house looked like her old, threadbare, faded overalls. She wondered if the old boards kept any of the dust out when the wind blew. A wrinkled, red haired, hound dog lay on the porch flapping his tail across a space where broken boards were gone. The door hung open.

Mr. Crenshaw turned the engine off and got out of the car. Maggie jumped out to follow Mr. Crenshaw toward the house. A man pushed a double barrel shotgun out of the door to scout the trail in front of him and sauntered to the edge of the porch. He held the gun balanced in the crook of his arm. His other hand hung limply through his overall strap and dangled in front of his bib. "Howdy, Crenshaw." He spat a stream of tobacco juice that landed by the hound.

"Morning, Stub."

"Come about the note?"

Mr. Crenshaw nodded. "It's due, Stub. Fact is, it's over due."

Mr. Huggins dragged his hand over his grizzly chin. "Ain't been no rain."

"I know, Stub."

"Ain't no money."

"I know."

"Might be some money comin' in."

"When?"

Mr. Huggins shrugged his shoulders. "Whenever Gatlin pays me."

"Mr. Gatlin hired you?"

"Yep."

"What did he hire you to do, Stub?"

Mr. Huggins looked long into Mr. Crenshaw's face. "Said it was secret. If I let it slip, I wouldn't get paid."

Maggie heard a whimper and looked behind Mr. Huggins. A dirty faced boy, probably six or seven years old, peeked out the door. Quickly a hand reached out and snatched him from the doorway. "Pa told us to stay out of the way in case there was shootin'!"

The air was thick with the words. Maggie looked at the double barrel again. If there was shooting, Mr. Huggins would have to be the one to start it. He was the only one with a gun.

"Stub, there is no need of shooting," Mr. Crenshaw spoke.

"There ain't nobody gonna take my land, Crenshaw." Mr. Huggins raised the shotgun ever so slightly, but there was no question in Maggie's mind that he would use it.

The hound dog raised his head with a low, warning growl.

"Stub, you have three days. Three days and then I need payment on your note."

"If Gatlin pays me, you'll get your money. If he doesn't, you'll have to wait, but you won't take my land." Mr. Huggins shot another stream of tobacco juice, this one landing just in front of Mr. Crenshaw's feet.

"Three days, Stub. The next time I'll have the sheriff with me."

"Get off of my land, Crenshaw!" This time Mr. Huggins aimed the shotgun at Mr. Crenshaw. It blasted into the ground where the tobacco stream had landed, sending a cloud of dust sparked with fireballs of shot.

Mr. Crenshaw yelled, "Get in the car, Maggie!"

The gun boomed again. Shot and dust stung Maggie. She turned, ran and dove into the car without the help of an open door.

Mr. Crenshaw started the engine and smashed the gas pedal to the floorboard. The car swerved and Maggie thought it must be balancing on two wheels. Maggie grabbed the dashboard and held on for dear life. The auto fishtailed up the drive, and almost rammed into one of the dead evergreens. Maggie slammed her eyes shut. Her heart raced faster than the car was going.

"Maggie, are you all right?" Mr. Crenshaw yelled over the pounding of the engine.

Maggie pulled her eyes open. Still she clutched the dashboard. "I think so!" she shouted.

Mr. Crenshaw didn't take the shortcut. Maggie figured he didn't want to stop and open the gate. She was glad. She needed all the time she could get to start breathing the right way again. A couple of miles down the road Mr. Crenshaw slowed down.

"I'm sorry about that, Maggie. I shouldn't have taken you to Stub Huggins' place."

"That's okay." Maggie smiled. It really was okay. At least she wasn't listening to Mrs. Crenshaw bark orders and working herself to the bone. Just wait until she told Opal and Pearl. Maggie peeked at Mr. Crenshaw. Being a banker must not be just an easy, sit-down, eight-to-five desk job!

CHAPTER 8

Banking

When the sedan stopped in front of the bank, Mr. Crenshaw laid his head on the steering wheel. He gulped a couple of deep breaths of air before he turned to Maggie. "If your daddy finds out about Stub Huggins taking a shot at you, he won't let you come to work for me again. I surely am sorry, Maggie. The truth of the matter is I thought if there were a little girl with me, Stub would tend to be nicer. I dreaded going out there. I don't like that kind of confrontation."

"My daddy won't find it out from me," Maggie promised. She needed the job too badly to have Daddy know what happened this morning. She would never tell. "Is Mr. Huggins a farmer?" She knew there had been no rain, so there wouldn't be any crops, but she hadn't seen any fields either.

Mr. Crenshaw laughed. "Stub? A farmer? I suppose he is if you could call moonshine a crop."

"He's a moonshiner? A bootlegger?"

"Well, no one has ever found his still, but plenty have found his crop." Mr. Crenshaw chuckled.

"Doesn't he know moonshine is against the law?"

"I'm pretty sure he knows it's against the law, but I'm pretty sure he doesn't care." Mr. Crenshaw laughed.

"He doesn't care?"

"Maggie, have you ever seen him in church?"

"No."

Mr. Crenshaw rubbed his chin. "Then maybe he doesn't know it is wrong, but more than likely he doesn't want to hear that it is wrong. These times are hard. It makes some people dishonest just to survive."

"Not my daddy," Maggie whispered.

"Well, Maggie, I am sure your daddy knows the Lord. He and Stub Huggins are very different."

Maggie thought about that. She began fruit inspecting again. First Stub Huggins had shot at both of them. Now she had found out he was a moonshiner. She felt sure Stub Huggins didn't have God in his heart.

Mr. Crenshaw opened the door and stepped into the street. He stuck his head back through the window. "Maggie, I think I need a bit of a break. Let's go to the drugstore and get us a fountain drink."

Maggie had never had a fountain drink in her whole life. She had heard they were wonderful, and she couldn't wait to tell Opal and Ruby. She slipped out of the car and walked beside Mr. Crenshaw.

They stepped up on the wooden porch of the drugstore. The door jingled when it swung open. Maggie followed Mr. Crenshaw to the counter and climbed up on a red metal, swivel stool.

"Morning, Mr. Crenshaw. What can I do for you?"

"Earl, we need a couple of sodas. This young lady has been working pretty hard this morning." Mr. Crenshaw winked at Maggie.

"Sure thing. Reckon we will see any rain soon?"

"I think everyone is praying we will, Earl. It sure would make my job easier. I don't like foreclosing on folks. That has to be one of the worst things about banking." Mr. Crenshaw looked grim.

"I've known some bankers who like it." Earl set the sodas in front of his customers.

Maggie heard nothing else. The soda glass had scallops scooped around the top, and it had a stem. She wrapped her hands around the tall, icy glass and pulled it toward her. She clamped her lips about the straw. Fizz splattered her nose as she took a long pull. Maggie came up coughing and sneezing together. Soda stung all the way down! She wondered if it was like moonshine. She had heard that moonshine burned clear to the toes. Maggie tipped her head. Opal had probably been the one who had said that, and Maggie was sure Opal had never tasted the stuff. She slurped on the straw again. The tingle felt great. Just wait until she told Opal and Ruby.

"What about that Sam Daniels?"

Maggie stopped drinking and began listening.

"What do you think about Thomas Gatlin taking him under his wing like that?" Earl asked.

"This here is his girl, Earl," Mr. Crenshaw swiveled his stool toward Maggie. "Maggie Daniels, this is Earl Morgan."

Earl held out his hand to Maggie. "Glad to meet you, Maggie."

Maggie shook.

The door burst open, its bell dancing. The same lanky boy who had delivered the yard goods to Maggie's house the night before rushed to stand beside them. "Mr. Crenshaw, sir, the lady who works at the bank sent me to find you. They need you right away." He was breathing hard.

"What happened?"

"Begging your pardon, sir, Mr. Crenshaw; they just sent me to get you. They didn't tell me what was the matter."

"Okay. Thanks, Willie." Mr. Crenshaw turned to Maggie. "Shall we head to the bank?"

Maggie thought her world was falling apart. She hadn't even half finished her soda, and she had to leave it sitting there on the counter.

Earl watched Maggie and chuckled. "Maggie, why don't you take the soda with you. You can finish it on your own time, and bring back the glass later."

"But it's glass, and it is beautiful. What if I break it?"

Earl leaned over the counter and whispered to Maggie. "I'll charge it to Mr. Crenshaw's account. After all, he runs the bank!"

"I heard that, Earl!"

Earl slapped the counter and laughed.

"I guess I'll be taking my soda, too." Mr. Crenshaw grabbed his glass.

"Go right ahead. I got your tab right here." Earl pointed to his head.

Maggie liked the way they joked with each other.

"Well, Maggie, you and I had better get out of this place before Earl charges my account for something else." Mr. Crenshaw held his glass high, turned and walked to the door.

Maggie's grin was loaded with thanks. She slid off the stool and followed Mr. Crenshaw.

"We'll just leave the sedan here and walk." Mr. Crenshaw didn't talk anymore.

Maggie wondered if he was worried about why they might need him at the bank. She squinted up at him, but she couldn't tell.

When they reached the bank, Mr. Crenshaw paused, closed his eyes and took a deep breath. "Maybe he is praying," Maggie thought as she closed her eyes, too.

Before the bank door even opened, a booming voice belched, "I want the banker now! Just where is Crenshaw!"

"Maggie, stay close to me. Be my shadow, but stay out of the way." Mr. Crenshaw opened the door and walked into the war zone.

Everyone stood stone still except for Mr. Thomas Gatlin. His face was red clear up to his hairline. His fists were clenched. Maggie thought his tie looked as limp as a summer dog's tongue. His eyes fell on Mr. Crenshaw. "Where in the world have you been?"

"On bank business, Thomas."

"Bank business is at the bank. I came in here on a matter of the utmost importance. I want to see you in private, and I want to see you now!"

"That would be fine, Thomas. Come on back to my office."

Mr. Thomas Gatlin turned and led the way. Maggie shadowed Mr. Crenshaw just the way he had said to do. Everyone in the bank made a wide aisle for them. Mr. Gatlin started his private discussion before the door even closed. "I want to know if my mother or my father had a safety deposit box."

Maggie slipped to the side, and Mr. Crenshaw closed the door.

Mr. Crenshaw walked over behind his desk and sat down. "Why?"

"What do you mean 'why'? They were my parents. I have a right to know. Did they, Crenshaw? Did they?" Mr. Gatlin leaned over the desk and stuck his nose within inches of Mr. Crenshaw.

Maggie pressed herself against the wall and close to the door.

"Sorry. That is a matter of privacy. It is protected information." Mr. Crenshaw didn't move.

"Private information? It is my family!" Like a striking snake, Mr. Gatlin's arm struck out and latched onto Mr. Crenshaw's neck, pulling him from the chair and across the desk.

Mr. Crenshaw growled and knocked Mr. Gatlin's hand away. He quietly stood upright. "Thomas, if you try that again, I will have the police called. If you want to discuss this, sit down away from me."

"Don't tell me to sit down! I won't. I can have your job for this. I own this bank! You will do what I tell you to do!" Maggie thought Mr. Gatlin was so hot you could fry an egg on his face.

"Thomas, you may think you own the bank. You may think you own me. You do not."

"Your job is gone!"

"You'll have to take it to the board of directors." Mr. Crenshaw stood his ground.

"Believe me, I will, but right now I want to know if my mother or father had a safety deposit box. I want you to tell me!"

"Thomas, I can't. It would be a breach of trust, and I won't do it. Go to the board of directors. They will stand behind me on this one. In fact, the law will stand behind me on this one."

"I'll get a lawyer!"

"Get one. It will take an act of law to make me break a trust, so you just go right ahead, Thomas." Mr. Crenshaw didn't budge an inch.

"You better believe I will. You just as much as told me what I needed to know. I want that deposit box, and I will get it with or without you." Mr. Thomas Gatlin backed away and swung around to go out the door. His eyes lit on Maggie.

Maggie froze and hoped she blended in with the wallpaper.

"What are you doing here?" He reached toward Maggie.

Maggie stumbled and her soda exploded into the air, drenching Mr. Gatlin. For a moment, he stood silently. Maggie thought she liked his noise better. He slid his hands over his face and flung soda rain. He gritted his teeth.

Mr. Crenshaw was around his desk and beside Maggie in three steps. "She is with me. Today she is learning a bit about banking."

"I suppose you are paying her?"

"That I am."

"I want her out of here! I want the whole lot of them gone!" Mr. Gatlin held both hands in fists.

"Thomas, I thought you were helping Sam Daniels and his family. That's what you announced at church on Sunday. You told the good people of Dodge City to come to their aid by charging things to your account for them. Just what did you have in mind?"

Maggie had slipped behind Mr. Crenshaw and listened to every word. She remembered Daddy had said Mr. Gatlin's gift was like the Trojan horse. Was it?

Mr. Thomas Gatlin slowly smiled. "I am being a help. I'm being a help to them and a help to myself."

"I don't know if they need your kind of help. I just wish I knew what was going on in that mind of yours." Mr. Crenshaw studied him.

"You'll find out soon enough." Mr. Gatlin craned his neck to see Maggie. "You talk your daddy into leaving the country. Tell him he'll go if he knows what is good for him and his family!"

Maggie shook.

"Thomas, I think you'd better leave." Mr. Crenshaw kept himself between Maggie and Mr. Gatlin.

Mr. Gatlin stomped to the door, yanked it open and slammed it behind him. Silence seemed to travel. Maggie didn't hear one single sound in the bank except Mr. Thomas Gatlin's angry footsteps.

Mr. Crenshaw turned and knelt in front of Maggie. "Are you all right?"

Maggie nodded. For the second time that day, Mr. Crenshaw had asked her that question.

"Have a seat." Mr. Crenshaw led her to a chair to sit down.

"Why does he hate my daddy?"

"I don't know. He sure hasn't been himself lately. Maybe it is because your daddy married Sue. A lot of people seem to think so. Maybe it's because his wife died. Sometimes that upsets a man."

"No one will give my daddy a job. It's because of him, isn't it?" Maggie wanted to cry. How could someone she didn't even know be an enemy?

"I expect so."

"Why do people listen to him? He isn't very nice. My daddy is nice."

"Maggie, it's not that those people don't like your daddy. They listen to Thomas Gatlin because most of them are in debt to him, and they know he will foreclose on them if they don't do what he says," Mr. Crenshaw explained.

"You don't listen to him."

Mr. Crenshaw smiled. "Oh, I listen to him. I just don't do what he tells me to do."

"Will he go to the board and get your job?"

"I imagine he will go to the board and try to get my job. Most of the people on the board are not in debt to him, so I am pretty safe."

"Good."

"Yes, that is good." Mr. Crenshaw went to his desk and sat with his elbows resting. He studied Maggie. "Maggie, has Sue ever said anything about things that are important to her?"

"You mean like Opal and Ruby and me and God and Daddy?"

Mr. Crenshaw rubbed his hand over his face and smiled. "Those things are very important, Maggie. You can learn a lot from Sue. You listen to her."

"I do." Maggie looked at the soda gathered in puddles on the hardwood floor. Her very first soda and she hadn't even gotten to drink it all. "Maybe I'd better go get something to clean this up."

"I'll get someone to do it. You just sit there." He glanced at his soda. "I'll tell you what, if you aren't afraid of drinking after me, I'd be glad to have you finish this off."

"I'm not afraid of you, Mr. Crenshaw." Maggie took the soda from him. She smiled as she remembered that only this morning she had been afraid of him because no one could find the Crenshaw shovel. Whoever owned the shovel, he couldn't be the one! He was one of the nicest people she knew.

Mr. Crenshaw came back in the office with a lady behind him. She had a mop and went right to work. Maggie hopped off the chair in time to save the straw the mop strings had caught. "I want to keep this." She held it high in the air. "Opal and Ruby will love it."

Mr. Crenshaw laughed. "You've had quite a day, haven't you?"

"Yes, sir. Banking is pretty scary business, and through all of this morning I haven't seen you sitting at your desk very much."

Mr. Crenshaw laughed. "I wish banking was only a desk job."

Whose Shovel?

There was a light tap at the door and a soft voice called, "Mr. Crenshaw?"

"Yes, Delta."

A chunky lady with her hair pulled back in a bun and her glasses balanced on the tip of her nose squeaked the door open. "Mr. Crenshaw?" she asked again.

"Come on in, Delta."

Delta squeezed in with a hasty look at Maggie.

"Delta, this is Maggie. She is my protégée. I'm teaching her banking today."

Maggie wondered what a protégée was. It sounded like some prehistoric dinosaur.

Delta's eyes slid Maggie's way with a slight smile. Quickly she turned back to Mr. Crenshaw. "I need to know just how to set up this account Mr. Gatlin wants to open for the Sam Daniels family.

"I don't know anything about an account, Delta."

Delta blinked. "Mr. Gatlin is setting it up now. I assumed he had been talking to you about it."

"What has he said about this account, Delta?" Mr. Crenshaw picked up a pencil and rolled it in his fingers.

"He wants it to be a special account for all the charges the Daniels family will make in regard to his special offer of credit. He wants to keep it separate from his own account."

Mr. Crenshaw tapped the pencil in the palm of his hand. "Delta, let me set up this account. Tell Mr. Gatlin I'll be right there."

"Thank you, Mr. Crenshaw." Delta seemed relieved as she glanced at Maggie and slipped out the office door.

"Mr. Crenshaw, my daddy won't like it. He doesn't want a thing from Mr. Thomas Gatlin. He doesn't trust him." Maggie looked somberly at him.

Mr. Crenshaw laughed. "He made that pretty clear Sunday, Maggie. This will probably come to nothing, because your daddy won't ever use any of the credit."

"If it was left up to Daddy, that's the way it would work," Maggie spoke under her breath.

"Sue wants to use the credit?" Mr. Crenshaw closed his hand around the pencil and leaned across his desk towards Maggie.

Maggie shook her head. "It's not Sue. It's Mr. Gatlin. We keep having boxes and packages delivered to our house that none of us have ordered. Mr. Gatlin went around and had them sent to us."

"Did your daddy send them back?"

"He tried. Everyone told him they can't take them back because if they do Mr. Gatlin will take his business elsewhere."

"That could be a problem." Mr. Crenshaw leaned back in his chair.

"My daddy thinks it is a problem."

"Your daddy is a smart man. I'll see what I can do. Maggie, you stay here. I'll go talk to Thomas."

Maggie sat back in her chair and swung her feet. She took a sip of her soda. She fingered the other straw and decided two straws would be better than one. She dunked it in her soda beside the other and slurped.

"I don't care what you think, Crenshaw. I will open this account, and I will keep track of all the expenditures." Mr. Thomas Gatlin lost his composure again. His voice rumbled through the walls of the bank.

"Thomas, why don't you come into my office. Let's sit down and think about what you are doing before it's too late," Mr. Crenshaw soothed.

"I don't need you to tell me what I am doing. I know what I am doing. I just need you to tell that daffy woman to open the account and to work it in the way I explained it to her!"

"Thomas, let's go to my office."

Maggie grabbed her soda and slid out of the chair. No way did she want to be in the office again when those two men were talking. Once had been enough.

At the doorway Maggie stopped. The outer bank doors had burst open. Daddy rushed in followed by Sue and the girls. Opal and Ruby were crying. Panting and looking wild, Daddy shouted, "Where's Maggie?"

Everyone in the bank froze.

"Where's Maggie?" Daddy asked again, almost yelling.

Mr. Crenshaw stepped from behind Thomas Gatlin and crossed to Daddy. "Mr. Daniels, Maggie is right here in the bank."

"Where? Is she safe?"

When Secrets come Home

Mr. Crenshaw looked puzzled. "Mr. Daniels, Maggie is fine. She is in my office." He pointed toward his office.

Maggie stood in the doorway. "Daddy, I'm fine."

Daddy turned to focus on Maggie. In a few fast steps, he knelt in front of her. He looked her up and down. "Are you sure you are not hurt?"

Maggie squinted at Daddy. "Am I supposed to be hurt?"

Sue spoke, "Maggie, were you in any kind of accident?"

Maggie shook her head. "No." She thought about Stub Huggins shooting at her, but no way would she mention that.

Opal pushed her way to Maggie. "Some guy said you were hurt."

Maggie looked at Opal. She could see the fright in her puffy eyes. "Opal, I'm not hurt. I'm fine."

Opal threw her arms around Maggie. Ruby pulled away from Sue and did the same.

Daddy left them in their huddle for a moment. His eyes asked a question of Sue.

Sue shrugged.

Gently Daddy pried the girls apart and took a deep breath. "Opal, tell me again about this man who told you Maggie had been hurt."

Opal slid her chubby hands cross her cheeks and began. "Ruby and I were out at the cottonwood talking to Lulubelle. I was up in the tree trying to get Ruby up there, too."

"She wanted me to ride Lulubelle with her. I didn't want to," Ruby interrupted.

"Opal!" Sue looked horrified.

"I told you, Opal, Lulubelle isn't like a horse. She is nice, but not if you try to get on her back." Maggie pressed her hands on her hips.

Sue began tapping her foot. "Opal! You tried to ride Lulu-belle before? Maggie, you should have told me."

"Sue, this we can finish at home," Daddy interrupted.

Sue nodded.

Maggie was glad for the interruption. Just how she could get in trouble when she wasn't even there was a mystery to her.

"What we need to know is about the man." Daddy looked at Opal.

"Well," Opal closed her eyes to think a moment. "He wasn't really a man. At first when I saw him walking across the pasture I thought it was Cecil."

"Cecil?" Mr. Crenshaw's breath caught.

"It wasn't. When he got closer I could tell he wasn't Cecil, but he must be about Cecil's age."

"Had you ever seen him before?" Mr. Crenshaw began asking questions, too.

"Nope," Opal shook her head.

"What about you, Ruby? Had you ever seen him before?" Daddy asked.

Ruby shook her head.

"Girls, both of you. I want you to think really hard. Exactly what did he say?"

Opal scratched her head. "He said, 'You Maggie's sisters?' We both told him we were. Then he asked where our mama and daddy were. We told him you were up at the house. Then he laughed and said something about 'that ole boxcar!' I told him to go away, but he said he had an important message to give to us. So I asked if he wanted to come to the house to give it to you or mama. I told him we would take him there. He wouldn't budge. He kept looking at the house, and he started getting antsy. Finally he said, 'Well do you want to hear the message or not?' We told him we did. He said, 'Maggie's been in a terrible accident' and we had better head to Dodge quick if we wanted to see her before something worse happened. So I dropped out of that tree, grabbed Ruby and we ran to tell you and Mama."

"Where did the boy go?" Daddy wanted to know.

Opal and Ruby both shrugged.

"Are you sure you have never seen him before?"

"Positive." Opal searched her mind to make sure.

"Ruby?"

She shook her head.

"What about at church. Have you ever seen him there?" Sue asked.

"No," Opal bit her bottom lip.

Daddy sighed. "Opal, would you know him if you saw him again?"

"Yes." Opal was sure.

"Maybe." Ruby added.

Daddy stood. He combed his fingers through his hair. He looked about him. All business in the bank had stopped. Everyone was watching. Daddy turned to Mr. Crenshaw. "I'm sorry. It seems we busted up your bank."

Mr. Crenshaw took Sam's hand. "Sam, it's just a bank. Maggie is the important thing here. I understand, and I would have done the same thing."

Thomas Gatlin stepped into the picture. "I wouldn't have. Those two girls probably made up the whole thing."

"We did not!" Opal walked over to him and stared up at him.

Maggie was proud of Opal for standing up to Mr. Thomas Gatlin, but she worried about Daddy. She watched as he slowly turned to face Mr. Gatlin. Sue reached over and touched his arm. "Sam, why don't we take the girls and go home. Please?"

Daddy stood still for a moment, and then nodded.

Mr. Crenshaw stepped to block Mr. Gatlin. "Why don't you folks go ahead and take Maggie. She has had quite a morning learning the banking business." Mr. Crenshaw pulled out his watch. "My goodness. It's past lunch and Maggie hasn't had anything to eat yet."

"We'd love to take Maggie. Thank you, Mr. Crenshaw." Sue took Maggie's hand in one of hers, and shook Mr. Crenshaw's hand with the other.

Mr. Crenshaw walked them through the door and followed them to the wagon. "Sam, if you find out who that boy was, let me know. I'll help in any way I can."

"Thanks, Mr. Crenshaw." Sam stretched out his hand.

"Arnold. You can call me Arnold." Mr. Crenshaw took his hand.

"Arnold." Sam smiled.

Maggie and Opal scrambled over the edge of the wagon. Maggie reached down to give Ruby a hand.

Opal turned to Sue. "Can we go to the store and just look around?"

Sue laughed. "No, Opal. Remember, we left everything topsy-turvy when we came storming in to town to check on Maggie. I hope I turned the beans off."

"But we never get to stay in town and just look around. There are some stores I have never even been in before." Opal wailed.

"You'll live." Sue smiled.

Opal slid on the straw. Her foot kicked the shovel. She picked it up and looked at it. "Mama, maybe we should go by Dr. Nelson's office and have him look at Maggie's chin."

"No, Opal. It's been too long. There's not a thing Dr. Nelson could do now unless he cut open the wound and sewed it up." Sue laughed. "We are going home."

Maggie groaned with the thought of pain. Opal groaned because her plan was foiled. She let the shovel fall. The handle crashed against the back of the wagon, slicing the air between Mr. Crenshaw and Daddy.

Silence broken only with terrified heartbeats was followed by a tiny screech. "I'm sorry!" Opal's eyes were huge.

"Opal." Daddy's voice held like a cracked dam.

Mr. Crenshaw laughed nervously. "That was close. I felt it whistle past my nose. Shakily he rested his hand on the shovel handle.

"Opal, apologize to Mr. Crenshaw," Sue ordered.

Opal turned her drained face to Mr. Crenshaw. "I'm sorry, Mr. Crenshaw."

"That's all right, Opal. No one was hurt. I'm fine." Mr. Crenshaw patted the shovel handle without thinking. He began tracing his finger around the blue stripe of the shovel handle. When he realized what he had done, he quickly pulled his hand away and stared. "Well, what do you know? I didn't think I would see another shovel like mine in all of Kansas!"

"That's like your shovel?" Daddy asked quietly.

Mr. Crenshaw nodded.

Daddy wadded up his fist and smacked Mr. Crenshaw in the nose. Mr. Crenshaw tumbled in a heap on the boarded sidewalk.

CHAPTER 10

Pressing Charges?

"Sam!" Sue dove off the wagon and ran to stand in front of Daddy. "What are you thinking?"

Maggie's head spun in circles. The shovel belonged to Mr. Crenshaw. Could he be the one who had thrown it at her? She tried to see her memory from the dark in a better light. Could that shadowy figure have been Mr. Crenshaw? Maybe. It could have been Daddy, too. At first, she thought it had been Daddy. Maggie swallowed. It could have been Mr. Crenshaw. Maybe he had taken her today to Stub Huggins in hopes he would kill her. Maggie shook her head. Mr. Crenshaw wouldn't have done that. He was her friend, and she believed in him. She remembered when he had first stood up for her against Mrs. Crenshaw. He had bought her the very first soda she had ever had. No. Mr. Crenshaw could not have been the one who threw that shovel.

"Sam! Sam!" Sue kept calling his name. She grabbed his arm and shook it. "Sam, why did you do that?"

"Didn't you hear him, Sue? He said that shovel belongs to him. He could have killed Maggie!"

"Get the sheriff! Someone get the sheriff!" Mr. Thomas Gatlin ordered.

Daddy twisted his arm free from Sue and went to stand in front of Thomas Gatlin. "Yes. By all means. Someone get the sheriff!"

Mr. Gatlin took a step backward. "Hurry! This man has gone crazy!"

"You may think I am a crazy man, Gatlin, and that is fine by me! You just keep on with this credit junk you are trying to pull, so people in Dodge City will think you're a nice person, and you'll see just how crazy I am!"

Mr. Thomas Gatlin backed up a step.

Mr. Crenshaw began moaning.

Daddy turned to pull him up and shove him against the back of the wagon. "So this is your shovel?"

Mr. Crenshaw blinked.

Daddy pulled his fist back.

Sue grabbed his arm. "Sam, don't!"

Daddy yanked his arm away from Sue. "He could have killed Maggie!" Daddy shouted again.

Maggie spilled over the edge of the wagon and ran to squeeze between the two men. "Daddy, he didn't do it!"

"Arrest that man!" Thomas Gatlin pointed Daddy out to the sheriff. "He attacked Arnold, and he has gone plumb out of his head."

Daddy let go of Mr. Crenshaw and turned toward Mr. Gatlin.

"Hold on, Thomas." The sheriff eased himself between Mr. Gatlin and Daddy. "Mr. Daniels, let's come over here, and we'll have us a talk."

"Sheriff, I am pressing charges. Sam Daniels needs to be put away." Thomas Gatlin pointed.

"Thomas, calm down. Maybe you had better go get yourself a cup of coffee," the sheriff suggested.

"And leave the scene of the crime? No way. I am an eyewitness. I can tell you right now what happened here. Arnold offered his hand to shake, and that crazy Daniels slugged him. He knocked him out cold for no reason at all. I am pressing charges." Thomas Gatlin paced back and forth.

The sheriff sighed. "Mr. Gatlin, you can't press charges. The crime was not committed against you."

"I most certainly can. I saw it all."

"That makes you a witness. It doesn't make you the victim. The victim is the one who can press charges."

"It happened in my town. I saw it. I want this man off the streets. I want this man arrested. I want him behind bars!" Gatlin stormed.

"Mr. Gatlin, it is not up to you." Still the sheriff kept himself between the two men. "Why don't you consider that cup of coffee."

"I will have your job for this." Thomas Gatlin spat.

"Mr. Gatlin, maybe you'd better make it two cups of coffee." The sheriff smiled.

"You'll never wear that badge again." Gatlin warned.

"Coffee, Mr. Gatlin, can be had in the town jail. I make a good cup. If you don't calm down, that is where your next cup of coffee is going to come from." The sheriff smiled, but his smile didn't quite reach his eyes.

"Why, you …"

The sheriff didn't let him finish. "Thomas, leave now. If I need your statement, I will find you."

Mr. Thomas Gatlin sputtered, turned and shoved his way through the crowd that had gathered.

He reminded Maggie of a firecracker on the Fourth of July. His fuse fizzled out before he blew, but some day he would explode almighty fast. When that happened, the firecracker would blow itself apart. Sure, it would hurt anyone close enough, but mostly it would hurt itself.

The sheriff shook his head as he watched Mr. Gatlin go. He turned to Mr. Crenshaw and Daddy. "Why don't we mosey over to my office and see if we can make heads and tails of this. We seem to have drawn quite a crowd here." He didn't even wait for an answer. He just expected them to follow.

Maggie looked at Daddy. He had calmed down a lot. Sue still took his arm, but Daddy grabbed the shovel with his other hand. Maggie didn't ask if they should go. She motioned for the girls to follow her. She needed to be there to help explain what happened.

The sheriff had Daddy sit across the room from Mr. Crenshaw and gave them both a cup of his coffee before he started. Maggie was glad Mr. Thomas Gatlin had gone somewhere else for his coffee. The sheriff handed a cup to Sue, poured a cup for himself, sat at his desk and began. "Who wants to be first?"

No one volunteered. The sheriff looked from one man to the other. He decided to start with Sue. "Sue, tell me what happened."

She paused, and then began, "Sheriff, I really don't know. We walked out of the bank together. Mr. Crenshaw and Sam were talking. Mr. Crenshaw had told us he would help us in any way he could. They shook hands. Mr. Crenshaw told Sam to call him Arnold, and the next thing I knew, Sam punched him."

"Sue, were there any words between them?"

Sue shook her head. "If you mean fighting words, no. Nothing that I heard."

The sheriff nodded his head. "Thank you, Sue. How about you, Arnold?"

Arnold shook his head. "I honestly don't know what happened. One minute we were friendly and the next thing I knew, I woke up on the ground."

The sheriff latched his hands around his neck and stretched. He leaned back in his chair and turned his eyes on Daddy. "Well, Sam? It seems it's up to you."

Daddy held up the shovel. "He said this shovel belongs to him."

"I said it is like mine." Mr. Crenshaw corrected.

"You slugged him over a shovel?" The sheriff put his hands on his desk and leaned forward in his swivel chair.

"Well, there aren't too many like that," Daddy began.

"I didn't say it is mine. I said I have one like it." Mr. Crenshaw held his hands palms out.

"You slugged him over a shovel?" the sheriff repeated.

Maggie thought the sheriff had started to think Daddy was crazy, too. "Mr. Sheriff," Maggie began.

The sheriff swung his eyes around to Maggie. "Do you know what happened, young lady?"

Maggie nodded, "I think so."

"Then let's have it."

"It really started last Friday night. I couldn't sleep, so I went to watch the night sky out my window. I do that sometimes, and I ask the God up in heaven to tell my mama 'hi' and that I miss her. Then I heard some kind of digging noise. I sneaked outside to see what it was. I followed the sound, which came from behind the cow shed. I got brave enough to peek around the corner, and I saw a man digging. It was real shadowy and dark, so I couldn't see him very well. At first, I thought it might be Daddy. I stepped out and asked him what he was doing. Well, it wasn't Daddy, but some other man. I guess I scared him because he turned and threw that shovel at me. I ran to the house and told Mama and Daddy."

"Is that right, Sam?" the sheriff asked.

Daddy nodded. "I found where it looked as if maybe someone had been digging. It could have been a coon though. We didn't find the shovel until Sunday, when we found it in the back of the wagon. I don't know who put it there or why. It is not my shovel. The thing is that shovel just missed Maggie's head. Sheriff, it could have killed her!"

The sheriff turned to Mr. Crenshaw. "Arnold? Is it your shovel?"

Mr. Crenshaw's eyes were wide. "I have one like it, but mine should be at home."

Maggie stepped over to stand beside Mr. Crenshaw. "I think it is his shovel."

"Maggie!" Mr. Crenshaw exclaimed, shocked. "Honey, I would never hurt you."

Maggie looked to the sheriff. "I don't think Mr. Crenshaw threw the shovel, but I do think it is his shovel."

"Why do you think that, Maggie?" the sheriff asked.

"Because Cecil and Elbert have been looking all over for Mr. Crenshaw's shovel and they can't find it," Maggie told him.

"They can't?" Mr. Crenshaw swallowed.

"Could it have been Cecil or Elbert who threw the shovel?" the sheriff asked.

Maggie shook her head. "It was a man. That much I know."

Daddy looked squarely at Mr. Crenshaw. "Crenshaw?"

Mr. Crenshaw shook his head. "You have got to believe me. I would do nothing to hurt Maggie. She has been the best thing that has ever happened in our home."

Mr. Crenshaw's and Daddy's eyes met and locked.

"Daddy, I believe him." Maggie patted Mr. Crenshaw's hand.

"Thank you, Maggie." Mr. Crenshaw seemed close to tears.

"Please, Daddy?" Maggie whispered.

Daddy lowered his eyes. "Okay, Maggie, I'll believe him, too. I'll trust your judgment." Daddy stepped across the room and held out his hand to Mr. Crenshaw. "Sorry, Mr. Crenshaw."

Mr. Crenshaw and Daddy shook hands. "Arnold. Please call me Arnold, and I'll help in any way I can."

"I guess this means you will not be pressing charges?" the sheriff asked.

Mr. Crenshaw laughed, "No. If I thought someone did that to my daughter, I would do the same."

"No charges? Well, that will make one Thomas Gatlin very unhappy." The sheriff chuckled.

"Will he have your job?" Maggie asked.

"Maggie, some days I would gladly give it to him." The sheriff laughed. When he saw that she didn't, he smiled. "Maggie, Mr. Thomas Gatlin thinks because he has a lot of money he owns Dodge City, but Dodge City has some very good people who can't be bought. Oh, things have pretty much gone his way. Lately he seems to be crossing some lines that he shouldn't. I don't think everybody will follow him across those lines. Maggie, he may try to take my job. I don't think the people of Dodge will stand for it."

"But no one will hire my daddy because of him."

Everyone seemed to be listening for the sheriff's answer. He sighed and leaned back in his chair. "I'm sorry about that. There may still be a job out there somewhere. Surely someone is brave enough to give your daddy a job."

"My daddy is leaving Friday," Maggie whispered.

Silence clung like a wet blanket over the room. Things were still the same. Daddy still had no job. No one in the room had any answers.

Opal and Ruby reached out and grabbed Daddy's hands. Sue studied the calendar on the wall above the sheriff's desk.

The sheriff broke the silence. "Sam, why would someone be digging on your property?"

Daddy shrugged. "I don't know."

"Sue? You have any buried treasures?" the sheriff asked.

"I wish," she laughed. "If I did, I'd be out there digging, too."

"Well, that's a puzzle." The sheriff drummed the top of his desk with his fingers. "You folks headed home since Arnold didn't press charges?"

Opal answered, "Yes! I wanted to go to the stores!"

"Opal!" Sue scolded.

"Mind if I follow you and snoop around. It seems if someone is digging around your place there must be a reason for it."

"Sheriff, we'd be glad to have you check it out," Daddy answered.

The sheriff walked over to the door and started to open it. He stepped back and shook his head. "Got a spectator. That Thomas Gatlin don't give up." The sheriff nodded his head to point across the street to where Mr. Gatlin waited. The sheriff sighed. "I wish he would have gone home to get that coffee. Tell you what. You go on home while I take care of Gatlin, and then I'll be along. Oh, and it would be a good idea to say nothing to anyone about the digging. I'd hate for someone to know we're on their trail," he winked.

Maggie studied Mr. Thomas Gatlin. His lips were in a grim line as he watched the Daniels family load up. His face turned almost purple when Mr. Crenshaw smiled and waved to them. As Daddy started the team, Mr. Gatlin made a beeline to the sheriff's office. Maggie wondered just how long Mr. Gatlin would take in the sheriff's office. The sheriff might not make it out to the Daniels' home today.

The bumpy ride jiggled Maggie's insides. Daddy and Sue were talking about the sheriff and all the things that had happened. Sue grabbed Daddy's arm and turned to him. "Sam, we didn't tell the sheriff why we were in town."

"I completely forgot."

"Do you think we should go back and let him know?" Sue asked.

Daddy paused a moment. "No. He said he'd be coming out. We can tell him about it then."

"Why do you suppose someone wanted us to think something bad had happened to Maggie?"

"I don't know, Sue. The girls said it was a boy. Maybe it was just a kid's prank." Daddy shrugged.

"You think so?"

"Could be."

"Sam, you don't really think so, do you?" Maggie could hear the worry in Sue's voice.

"I think we'd better keep a close eye on Maggie."

"Maggie," Ruby tugged at the hem of her dress.

Maggie's attention turned to the girls. "What?"

"Opal says there must be hidden treasure somewhere around the cow shed." Ruby's eyes sparkled.

Opal nodded. "It makes sense. I started thinking about that when the sheriff asked about hidden treasure on the place. If someone is digging, there must be a reason why. There has got to be something valuable, something so important that someone is looking for it!"

"Opal thinks we should start digging for it, too. She thinks we should start tonight after Mama and Daddy are asleep!" Ruby whispered.

"Why? If there is something important, Mama and Daddy might be able to help us." Maggie stopped. The color drained from her face. She felt cold all over. "Something important," she whispered.

"Are you okay?" Opal asked.

Maggie nodded her head in a lie. How could she be okay? She had just remembered sitting in Mr. Crenshaw's office, when he asked her if Sue ever talked about things that were important to her. Had Mr. Crenshaw looked for something that was important to Sue? Could Mr. Crenshaw have thrown the shovel at her? She rubbed her hands together and licked her lips. She had convinced Daddy to believe in Mr. Crenshaw. Had she made a mistake? Would she regret that mistake?

Treasure!

aggie squeezed her face between her hands. She had to find a way that would help her to know if Mr. Crenshaw was her friend or her enemy. Her heart told her he was a friend. The evidence could be telling her he was her enemy. She couldn't go on this way. Maggie stole a sliding glance at Daddy and Sue. They would know, but if she told them the suspicious facts, Maggie felt they wouldn't let her go to work with Mr. Crenshaw anymore. Maggie shook her head. She couldn't tell them. Opal and Ruby? No. Opal and Ruby would tell Daddy and Sue whether they meant to or not. Maggie closed her eyes. "Dear God up in heaven …" That was it! Pastor Olson had taught that on Sunday. He had said you shall know them by their fruit. Maggie could be a fruit inspector again. She reached deep into her pocket and pulled out a folded piece of paper where she had written the fruit of the spirit. Let's see, did Mr. Crenshaw have love? Yes.

Joy? Yes. Sometimes he even laughed at the things that made Mrs. Crenshaw mad.

Peace? Maggie thought about that one. Did Mr. Crenshaw have peace? He seemed peaceful when Stub Huggins got upset. He shook a little after Stub shot at him. Probably anyone would shake after that. Maggie smiled. She had shook, thinking she might have a heart attack because her heart pounded clear up in her throat. Mr. Crenshaw had seemed pretty peaceful when Mr. Gatlin yelled at him, and he didn't seem worried that Mr. Gatlin could take his job. Peaceful? Maggie would have to say "yes" on that one.

Longsuffering? Maggie giggled. Sue had told her that meant putting up with something annoying for a long time and not getting mad. Mr. Crenshaw definitely had longsuffering. He was married to Mrs. Crenshaw.

Gentleness? He was pretty gentle when he talked to her and Cecil and Elbert, and even Mrs. Crenshaw. Goodness? Yes. He hated to go tell Stub Huggins the bank needed a payment.

Faith? Maggie nodded. She felt sure he had faith.

Meekness? Sue had said it meant a person was well trained to do a job, any job the Lord might ask them to do. Maggie thought about that. She wasn't sure exactly. If God wanted him to be a banker, she guessed he was well trained. She didn't know if it meant he was a well-trained Christian. Now Mrs. Valina was, and Sue was, too. They talked about the Lord and that He should be in your everyday life. Maggie knew she had the God up in heaven in her heart, just as Sue had taught her. Mrs. Valina had told her about heaping coals of kindness on her enemies, so she could endure them and maybe they would even become her friends. It worked. Elbert had become her friend. Maggie shrugged. She couldn't really be sure about Mr. Crenshaw. She looked at the last one on her list.

Temperance? Sue had said it was the hardest of all. It meant to have self-control. Maggie laughed out loud. Today someone had shot at Mr. Crenshaw, yelling at him and threatening his job, and Daddy had smacked him in the face and sent him flying. Maggie hadn't seen Mr. Crenshaw get mad once. The answer to whether he had temperance would have to be "yes." Maggie folded the paper and tucked it back in her pocket. Out of all those fruits, only one Maggie couldn't be sure Mr. Crenshaw had. She felt she should trust him. Someone else must have thrown the shovel. It couldn't have been Mr. Crenshaw.

Daddy pulled up to the house. "Girls, you go on in. Your mama and I will take the horses to the shed."

Maggie jumped to the ground. Opal and Ruby followed. "I got to go!" Ruby yelled as she flew around the side of the house toward the outhouse.

"Me, too!" Opal disappeared.

Maggie giggled. There sure was never a dull moment with sisters. She loved them even though they seemed to be getting her in trouble all the time. Maggie climbed the steps, opened the screen door and crossed the porch. It was good to be home early. She pulled the door open and froze. What a mess she saw! The kitchen cabinet stood with doors swung wide. All the food and dishes were scattered over the whole floor. Someone had ripped the calendar off the wall. The blanket that made the door for the girls' room lay in a heap. Maggie's heart pounded. Slowly she backed up.

Maggie could hear Opal and Ruby coming. She needed to stop them. She had to get Daddy. She closed the door and ran across the porch to meet Opal and Ruby. "Hey, the last one to the cow shed is a rotten egg!" she shouted.

There were no questions asked. Both girls turned and skedaddled. Maggie ran, too. She wanted to be away from that house. It felt sinister. Someone had been in there. What would happen if they were still there? Maggie ran faster. She looked behind to see if anyone followed her, and smacked right into Daddy.

"Whoa! Somebody after you?" he laughed.

Wildly Maggie shook her head.

Sue stepped in. "Sam, something is wrong. Maggie is shaking."

"Maggie?" Daddy asked.

Between gasps Maggie answered. "Someone … in … the … house!"

"Now?" Daddy ran. "Sue, stay with the girls!" He shouted over his shoulder.

"Sam, be careful!" Sue called, but Daddy had already gone. She wrapped her arms around Maggie. Together they stood stone still. Only their throbbing hearts hinted they were alive. Opal and Ruby huddled together at their feet. The screen door slammed. No one dared to move, and each strained to hear anything from the house. Time seemed to be holding its breath, too.

Footsteps walked into the silence. The screen door screeched, and Daddy stepped out from the porch. Slowly he sat down on the top step.

Maggie pulled herself from Sue and sped toward Daddy, kicking up little dust clouds from under her feet as she ran across the dry grass. Maggie threw herself into Daddy's arms.

Sue followed Maggie. "Sam?"

Daddy shook his head. "No one is in there now, but someone sure had a heyday. I don't think anything is torn up, but everything is sure messed up."

"Why?"

"It appears someone was looking for something." Daddy spoke. "Sue, is there anything important that you have?"

Sue furrowed her brow. "Sam, you know what I have." She spread her arms. "Nothing. I have nothing important but you and the girls."

"I don't understand." Daddy's voice became quiet.

"Hey! The sheriff is coming!" Opal announced.

"Good." Daddy stood to wait for him.

The sheriff stopped, stepped out of the car and studied them. "Something wrong?"

Daddy strode over. "I guess we had a visitor while we were in town."

"Oh? Why do you say that?"

"Come on inside, Sheriff." Daddy led the way. Sue and the girls followed.

Daddy opened the door and stood back to let the sheriff in. He took a couple of steps and paused.

Sue gasped, "Sam!"

Opal and Ruby buzzed by. Opal lurched to a stop. Ruby ran into the back of her. "Watch where you're going!" Opal warned. From there the girls raced to their room. "Hey! Someone dumped our drawers."

"And look at our bed." Ruby whistled.

Maggie followed. The bed was tipped up against the wall. The drawers were dumped, and the contents were strung over the bedroom floor. The carpetbag Maggie had used to stash all her mama's special treasures was empty, with everything strewn about the room. Maggie dropped to her knees beside the bag, and carefully began putting her treasures back into it.

"Wait."

Maggie stopped.

The sheriff stood at the door. "Before we do any cleaning, I need to look at everything. I need all of you to make sure there isn't anything missing. Don't put anything up until we know." He turned to Daddy and Sue, "Do you folks have anything valuable?"

Daddy and Sue looked at each other. "No."

"It looks as if someone thinks you do." The sheriff took his hat off and ran his fingers through his hair.

"Sheriff, we do need to tell you why we were in town today," Sue began.

The sheriff looked at Sue.

Daddy continued, "Opal and Ruby were playing out in the pasture when a boy told them Maggie had been in an accident, and we were needed in Dodge City to get her."

The sheriff nodded his head. "Someone wanted you all out of the house."

"It looks that way." Daddy scanned the room.

"Girls, who was this boy?" The sheriff directed his gaze at them.

"We don't know," Ruby answered.

"We never saw him before," Opal added.

"Are you sure?"

Both girls nodded.

"Well, I'll tell you what. You all check everything in here. If you find anything missing, you let me know. If you find something that wasn't here before, you let me know that, too." The sheriff slapped his hat against his leg, and set it back on his head. "I think while you do that, I'll go nose around outside. Sam, do you want to show me where that digging was?"

"Sure, Sheriff."

As the door shut, Sue sighed. "Opal, hand me my apron. Maggie, grab the broom. I think we have some deep cleaning to do. We can sweep under the beds really well since they are standing on end." Sue laughed.

Maggie handed the broom to Ruby. "Here, you sweep in here while I pick up all the clothes and put them back in our drawers." Maggie ducked into their bedroom and picked up her carpetbag. Slowly she examined each of her mama's things as she tucked them back into her bag. Maggie closed her eyes to bring up a picture of Mama. Sue's face came up instead. Maggie's eyes flew open. With panic, she closed them again. She could barely remember what Mama looked like. Maggie felt guilty. When had that happened? Wildly she dug for the one picture she had of Mama. She yanked it out and pressed it to her chest. Tears began to trickle down her face. Then like a spring cloudburst, the tears gushed. Maggie sobbed.

Opal started into the room. "Maggie?"

Maggie didn't hear her.

Opal backed away. "Mama, Maggie's crying."

Sue turned from the cupboard. She wiped her hands down her apron and crossed to the girls' room. Gently she sat on the floor beside Maggie and wrapped her arms around the little girl.

Maggie felt the warmth. It wasn't just body heat. It was warmth from the heart.

Sue rocked her back and forth and crooned. "It's all right, Maggie. It's okay."

Finally, Maggie sobbed, "It's not all right! I can't remember what my mama looked like! I have to look at her picture!"

"Oh, honey!" Softly Sue pulled the picture from Maggie's hands. She studied it. "Why, Maggie, look. You have your mama's eyes and her smile. You look just as beautiful as she does in this picture." Sue paused, "Maggie, anytime you want to see your mama, you just find a mirror, look into it and smile. Your mama will be smiling right back at you."

"Do you really think so?" Maggie whispered.

"I know so." Sue ran her finger down Maggie's cheek and under her chin. She tipped her face to look into her eyes. "Maggie, Margaret Pearl, let's have your daddy make a frame for this picture. Then we'll hang it on the wall wherever you want it!"

"Do you think it will bother Daddy?"

"No." Sue shook her head. "I know your daddy loved your mama. I don't think it will bother him at all. I think he will be glad you have this picture, and you want to see your mama."

Maggie lowered her eyes. "What about you? Will it bother you that my mama's picture is on the wall?"

Sue's eyes clouded, but her smile was sincere. "Honey, from everything I have heard about your mama I know she loved you and your daddy very much. She was a wonderful lady, and I would be proud to have her picture gracing my walls."

Maggie's arms slid around Sue. "Thank you, Mama," she whispered.

Opal came to the doorway and stood. "Mama," she whispered.

"Yes, Opal?"

"The tea is boiling."

"I'll be right there." Sue looked at Maggie. "Will you be okay?"

Maggie nodded. She slid her hands across her cheeks.

Sue stood. "Opal, why don't you go ask your daddy and the sheriff if they would like some tea."

Opal charged from the room. They heard the screen door slam and Sue shook her head. "Maggie, how about some tea?" She held out her hand to Maggie.

"That would be nice."

"My, don't you sound grown up?"

"Here they come!" Ruby yelled.

Sue and Maggie stepped into the room as Opal held open the door for the sheriff and Daddy. The sheriff carried a crate that he eased to the kitchen table. "I guess your midnight visitor wasn't digging for treasure. He was burying it."

The girls crowded around. Maggie watched Daddy's face. It held no smile.

"Wow! Treasure!" Ruby clapped her hands.

"I knew it! I knew it! I knew it!" Opal danced.

Sue, too, was watching Daddy.

The sheriff pulled out his pocketknife and began prying off the lid. When the lid popped back, Opal and Ruby shoved so close to the crate that the sheriff chuckled. "Back up there, girls."

"But I want to see." Opal wailed.

"Me, too. Please." Ruby pleaded.

"You'll all see in just a bit, but if it is something dangerous you won't want to be that close," the sheriff told them.

"Like a snake?" Opal plunged backwards.

"Well," the sheriff chuckled, "we'll find out."

The crate was packed with straw. Very carefully, the sheriff started pulling handfuls away. "Mm hmm, that's just what I thought this treasure might be." The sheriff pulled out a brown bottle with a cork shoved into the mouth of it. He took his pocketknife and worked at the cork until it shot across the room. Liquid spewed down the side of the bottle.

"Wow!" Opal whistled.

The sheriff held it to his nose and took a whiff. "Moonshine!"

"Moonshine?" Sue's eyes were big.

"What's moonshine?" Ruby asked.

"Illegal," Daddy whispered.

The sheriff put the bottle on the table, pulled out a chair and sat. "Sam, Sue, have a seat."

Both sat.

Maggie backed against the wall. Moonshine? Her pulse raced. "Are you going to arrest Daddy?"

The sheriff took a deep breath and kicked at some unseen object on the floor. "Maggie," he looked up at the ceiling, "that depends."

"My daddy didn't do it. He wouldn't do it." Maggie spread her hands against the wall.

"These are bad times, Maggie. They make people do wrong things," the sheriff quietly spoke.

"Not my daddy!" Maggie felt an echo in her ears. She had already said that once today. Maggie slid down the wall. Sue's Bible rested on the floor beside her. She picked it up and held it close. "Please, God up in heaven, be with my daddy!"

"I hope your daddy didn't do it, Maggie." The sheriff turned to Sam. "Sam, I have to ask you some questions." The sheriff tipped his hat back on his head.

Daddy nodded.

"Sam, are you bootlegging?"

Daddy's eyes never wavered. "No, sir."

"Is this crate of moonshine yours?"

"No, sir," Still Daddy stared at the sheriff.

"Do you know how it got on your property?"

"No, sir."

The sheriff turned to Sue. "Sue, are you bootlegging?"

"Sheriff! No, I am not!"

"I'm sorry, Sue. I didn't believe you were, but I did have to ask." He looked down for a minute, and then back at Sue. "Is the moonshine yours, and can you tell me how it came to be on your property?"

"No, sir, it is not mine, and I do not know how it got here."

"Well, that is what I figured. I think something is going on here, but I don't have it sorted out," he paused. "Sam, I'm going to have to ask you not to leave town until this is all settled."

Maggie's mouth fell open. Daddy couldn't leave town now. Maggie toyed with the ribbons that hung from the Bible. Was this an answer to her prayers? It seemed like a hard way to answer her prayers.

Daddy nodded. "I couldn't very well leave town anyway, not after someone went through the house. No telling what they might do next."

Sue reached over and found Daddy's hand, "Thank you, Sam."

The sheriff seemed to be still studying the situation. He cleaned his fingernails with his pocketknife. Finally, he snapped it closed and shoved it into his pocket. He leaned on the table and looked at Daddy and Sue. "First, I want you to know I believe you. I also need the whole family to keep this under your hat."

Opal scrunched her face. "I don't have a hat."

The sheriff laughed.

"He means we are to keep all of this a secret, Opal. No one is to tell anyone what happened here today," Sue explained.

"But it's a good story." Opal complained.

"No. You can't tell anyone. Is that understood?" Sue asked.

"Yes, ma'am," Opal frowned. "I won't breathe a word."

"Good." Sue turned back to the sheriff.

"You are just to go on as though nothing happened at all. Everyone understand that?" The sheriff took turns looking each one in the eye and waiting for their agreement. "Now, Sam, I need you to keep an eye on things out here."

"Yes, sir."

"Sam, I am talking about keeping a legal eye on things here."

Daddy tipped his head to the side. "Legal?"

The sheriff nodded. "Legal. I guess that means I'll have to deputize you. Is that okay by you?"

Daddy's mouth dropped open.

"Sam will be a deputy?" Sue asked in awe.

"A secret deputy. I don't want anyone to know it yet. He'll be under cover, but I want him to have the authority to do whatever needs to be done if I'm not here."

"Sheriff, is this a paying job?" Sue whispered.

The sheriff nodded. "Sam, what do you say?"

"Yes, sir."

"You folks have a Bible around here?"

Maggie had the Bible in her arms. She scrambled to her feet and handed it to the sheriff.

The sheriff placed the Bible in the middle of the table. "Sam, put your left hand on the Bible, raise your right hand and repeat after me."

CHAPTER 12

Gunnysack

Maggie twirled and sang snatches of songs. It didn't matter what song. Any song would do. If she didn't know the words, she made them up. Maggie ran to the cottonwood tree in the middle of the pasture. She hugged the trunk. The rugged bark felt hard and scratchy against her face, and her arms didn't even reach half way around the trunk. She looked up into the dangling leaves. "Mr. Cottonwood, God gave my daddy a job! He doesn't have to leave and go work in the salt mines on Friday. He gets to stay with us." Maggie giggled because the breeze rustled through the cottonwood leaves as if they were answering her. She had needed to say that. She really needed to shout it. She wanted all of Dodge City to know, every single one of those people who wouldn't give her daddy a chance. She wanted all of them to know.

"Just wait until I tell Mrs. Valina!" Maggie yelled, and then she groaned. She was the one who would have to wait. The sheriff said they were to tell no one. How? Maggie remembered Pastor Olson saying something about praising God. If the lips of all the people in the world were sealed, the very grass of the earth would burst forth with praise for our Lord! That was exactly the way she felt. She would burst if she couldn't tell someone, but the sheriff had said to tell no one. No one meant that Maggie couldn't tell even Mrs. Valina. She would have to try to hide her excitement from Mrs. Valina. Just how could she do that? Mrs. Valina always knew when Maggie needed to talk about something. She even knew sometimes before Maggie knew she needed to talk. Maggie looked to the cloudless sky through the dancing cottonwood leaves. "Dear God up in heaven, you are going to have to help me keep this a secret."

"What secret would that be?" a quiet airy voice spoke from behind her.

Maggie had heard that voice before. She didn't remember where, but it sent chills up her spine. Slowly she let go of the rough bark and turned. Her heart started pumping faster, so fast it seemed to be roaring in her ears.

Stub Huggins grinned at her. "So you got yourself a secret?" He shot a stream of tobacco juice at her feet.

Maggie took a step backward and bumped into the trunk of the cottonwood.

Stub Huggins set the end of his double barrel on the ground and leaned toward her. "Just what might that secret be, girlie?"

Maggie pulled herself straight against the trunk and seemed to find some strength in the tree. "It would be none of your business."

"I'm makin' it my business, girlie. Now just tell ole Stub this secret." His mouth spread in an evil smile.

Maggie stepped from the tree. "If you will excuse me Mr. Huggins, I must go or I will be late for work."

Stub Huggins laughed. "You actin' kinda high and mighty, ain't you?"

Maggie started to walk past him.

Stub Huggins stuck the barrel of his shotgun across her chest. "You ain't goin' nowhere. We got some secrets to discuss."

Maggie looked across the pasture. It was too far for anyone to hear her if she screamed. It was too far to try to out run Stub Huggins. She licked her lips.

Stub read her mind. "Girlie, I wouldn't try it if I was you. I'd have you caught faster than a skunk can spray a coon dog! Yell all you want to; ain't nobody gonna hear you. You might as well get your mind set to the idea that you're comin' with me."

"Why? I am worth nothing. My daddy and mama have no money to pay anything for me. My daddy doesn't even have a job." Maggie spread her hands.

"Girlie, that ain't my problem. I'm just doin' what I have to do to get by. Now come on quiet like." Stub motioned with the double barrel.

Maggie looked in the direction he motioned. They would be crossing the Gatlin back pasture. Maybe Mrs. Valina or Martin would be out. She would go along with Stub Huggins until she was in shouting distance of the house, and then she would shout up a storm. She walked. With each step, she prayed. Mrs. Valina would be looking for her before long. She would have her basket of heaping coals ready to take to the Crenshaws. Cecil and Elbert would be watching for her, too. They waited for her and the basket of goodies she always brought.

Maggie looked up ahead. Martin was pounding iron at his blacksmith's shop. If they got close enough she could start yelling.

Stub Huggins nudged her in the back with the gun. "You'd better not do anything. I'd shoot him with this scatter gun as soon as I'd look at him."

Maggie sucked in her breath. How did he seem to know what she was thinking? Maybe if she just kept watching Martin he would look her way. Martin stopped pounding. Maggie strained her ears.

"Martin, you seen Maggie this morning?" Mrs. Valina called.

"Whoa, girlie."

Maggie stopped and whispered. "You can't shoot both of them."

"It's a double barrel," Stub Huggins hissed. "Besides, that's why I brought this." He waved a gunnysack.

Maggie stared. Stub Huggins pointed to Mrs. Valina swaying across the Gatlin drive towards Martin. Maggie followed his finger. Stub swung his double barrel and smacked Maggie in the back of the head. Maggie's legs crumbled beneath her. Vaguely she was aware of Stub shoving her into the itchy, dusty gunnysack. She felt him heft the bag over his shoulder. Maggie and the bag swung as he started walking. From far, far away she heard Mrs. Valina call. "Stub, you been hunting?"

"Yep, sure have."

"Looks like you had luck," Mrs. Valina commented.

"Sure did. Pretty good sized deer in here." Stub chuckled.

"Well, good for you. Stub, you seen a little girl?" Mrs. Valina asked.

"Nope." Stub lied.

Maggie couldn't move. She could hardly breathe. She wanted to shout, but if she did, Stub would shoot Mrs. Valina. There had to be another way. "Please, God!" she begged.

"Have yourself a fine day, Stub," Mrs. Valina called.

Maggie listened to Mrs. Valina's voice die away, and felt like all hope was dying, too. Her head hurt. Her body hurt. Her heart hurt. Was this the way her life would end? She hung upside down in an old, dirty gunnysack. Maggie began to panic. She started fighting at least to turn right side up.

"You want another knock on the skull?" Stub warned.

Maggie closed her eyes and quit struggling.

Finally.

Stub Huggins dropped the bag on the hard ground. "You can get yourself out now," he told her.

Maggie fought the gunnysack. She grabbed and pulled and tore at the burlap until she could see light. She ripped it off her head and looked around.

She wasn't surprised to be sitting in the middle of Stub Huggins' hard-packed dirt yard. The red hound dog moseyed over and sniffed Maggie. Maggie pushed him away and pulled herself to her feet. The gunnysack was tangled at her ankles. She stumbled and kicked it away.

Stub Huggins chuckled. "Didn't think you liked that over much."

"I didn't." Maggie brushed her hands down the side of her dress. "Just what are you going to do with me now?"

"Nothin'."

"Nothing? Nothing? Then why did you take me? That's kidnapping, and you can go to jail for kidnapping!" Maggie stomped.

"I hope not, because I ain't goin' to jail. You ain't kidnapped. You're just here to answer some questions." Stub leaned on the porch post.

"You took me when I didn't want to go. You hit me on the head and stuck me in that stinking gunnysack. You said you would shoot Martin and Mrs. Valina! You don't think you'll go to jail?" Maggie yelled.

"You want back in that sack?"

"No." Maggie looked down at it with horror.

"Then quiet it down," he paused. "You might as well come on over and sit whilst you wait." Stub pointed to the porch.

"What am I waiting for?" Maggie walked to the porch.

"The boss."

Maggie's skin prickled. Just who could the boss be? Why would anyone want her? What questions was the boss going to ask her? Would she know the answers?

The torn screen door slammed. A boy about Cecil's size walked over and stood watching her. "You want a biscuit?" He reached into his pocket, pulled one out and shoved it her way.

Maggie looked at the biscuit. It was falling apart and had been in his pocket. She didn't want the biscuit, but if this would make a friend she would take it, and she would eat it. "Thanks," she whispered.

"Jed, I don't want you makin' friends with that girl. As soon as the boss comes she'll be leavin'." Stub didn't even look around.

"Have you lived here long?" Maggie asked.

"All my life."

"Is your mama here?"

"Don't have one."

"Did she die?" Maggie's voice softened.

"Yep."

"I'll bet you miss her." Maggie's eyes clouded.

"Not much. She died when Jess was born. I was only two, so I didn't know her much." Jed kicked at the porch boards.

"I'm sorry she died, and I'm sorry you didn't get to know her. Mamas are pretty special. I miss mine a lot." Maggie gazed down the drive.

"Jed, I told you I didn't want you makin' friends. Now go keep Jess out of trouble." Stub was gruff.

Jed turned and tromped back into the house.

Maggie waited until he was out of sight. "Mr. Huggins, does Jed know what you are doing with me? Does he know you kidnapped me?"

"It ain't none of the boy's business. Besides, I'm between a rock and a hard place. I got to get money some way." Stub sat on the step. The red hound snuggled beside him and laid his head in Stub's lap.

"What about your moonshine business? Doesn't it make you money?" Maggie asked.

Stub pulled the lever on the shotgun. "What do you know about moonshine?"

"That it's illegal."

Stub spat his stream of tobacco juice. "That law shoulda never been made. Moonshine can be used for medicinal reasons. Seems it can be exactly what the doctor ordered."

"Are you a doctor?" Maggie asked.

Stub put a finger to the brim of his greasy hat and laughed "Why, I guess I am, girlie!"

"If you get caught, Mr. Huggins, you'll go to jail. If you go to jail, what will happen to Jed and Jess?" Maggie wanted to know.

"You better hope I don't get caught because if I do, I'll blow the whistle on your pa. If I go to jail, he goes to jail, too." Stub chuckled.

"Why would he go to jail?"

"I know where he's got a crate of moonshine hidden right under your nose! If I get caught I'll lead the sheriff direct to it!" Stub looked smug.

Maggie sucked in a deep breath. "You're the one who threw the shovel at me! You could have killed me!"

"If I had aimed to kill you, you'd be dead! I ain't missed nothin' since I was nigh on ten years old. I was just tryin' to scare you." Stub squinted his eyes at Maggie. "It worked, too. You ran faster than a horse in the Kentucky Derby!" He laughed.

Maggie couldn't disagree with what he had said. She had been scared half out of her wits. She still had some questions she wanted answered. She smiled. She was here because the boss had questions he wanted her to answer, and she was the one asking the questions. "Mr. Huggins, why did you put the shovel in the back of our wagon?"

Stub slapped his leg and laughed. "It threw everyone off the trail. There is only one person who has a shovel like that. That man is gonna foreclose on me. Just see if he can foreclose from a jail cell!"

"How did you get Mr. Crenshaw's shovel?" Maggie pushed a little more.

Stub nodded toward the house. "Jed. He's a good boy. He'll do what I tell him to do."

Maggie's stomach felt sick. It could be from the knot on her head, but she really thought it was because Jed was just a kid. His own daddy had him stealing. "Don't you feel bad about Jed stealing?"

"From Crenshaw? Crenshaw is trying to steal my place! What's a shovel compared to my place?" Stub reasoned.

Maggie shook her head. She didn't understand, and she sure didn't think Stub Huggins understood. "Why did you hide that crate of moonshine in our cow shed?"

Stub shrugged. "Boss told me to."

"Does the boss want my daddy to go to jail?" Maggie pried.

"Could be. I don't ask him the why of what he tells me to do."

Maggie was frustrated. "Don't you care if my daddy goes to jail for something he didn't even do?" Maggie smacked her hands down on the porch. The old hound dog lifted his head and growled.

"Whoa, Bert." Mr. Huggins patted the dog. "Girlie, you best talk nice around Bert. He don't take kindly to strangers anyway."

"Why do you think your boss wants my daddy to go to jail?" Maggie persisted. She rubbed her throbbing head.

"Girlie, I guess that's somethin' you can just ask him your own self because here he comes now." Stub pushed the hound off his lap and stood with the double barrel looped in his arm.

Maggie stared down the lane. Dust billowed so much she couldn't even tell the make of the automobile. Her heart raced against the pounding in her head. What questions did the boss want answered? Did he think Stub had kidnapped her? If he did, what would the boss want to do with her? Maggie stood twisting the sides of her dress and squinting to see if she knew the car.

Meeting the Boss

The auto screeched to a halt, but the huge plume of dust still swirled. Maggie held her breath as a suited man with a hat pulled low shadowing his eyes passed through the swirling cloud. It was eerie! Maggie shivered. He seemed to appear from out of nowhere. This was the boss. Maggie grabbed the porch rail to steady herself.

"Stub, you got it?"

Maggie recognized the voice before the dust cleared. It didn't do anything to make her feel better.

Stub rubbed the back of his neck. "Sort of."

"Sort of? Stub, either you got it, or you don't. What do you mean by sort of?" The voice strained against anger.

"I couldn't find it, so I got the girlie."

"The girl?" The very air seemed to crackle.

"Boss, I thought she could tell you what you need to know," Stub explained.

The boss cut loose with a few choice words. "Stub, do you know what it's called when you take a kid?"

Maggie stepped forward. "I can tell you what it's called: kidnapping!"

The boss took one look at Maggie, and ripped the hat from his head and threw it. The hat skipped across the dirt where Bert pounced, chomped and slung the hat wildly back and forth.

"Stub! You would have to get this one! Why couldn't you have gotten the little one! At least she might not have known me! This one! This one is going to cause trouble! She knows me!"

Maggie stepped off the porch and walked to stand in front of the boss. "Yes, I know you. You are going to go to jail, Mr. Thomas Gatlin! You are going to go to jail for kidnapping!"

Gatlin stared. Like lightning, he snatched Maggie by the arm. "I will not go to jail. I didn't take you. Stub did!"

"Stub did it for you. That's the same as doing it yourself." Maggie shook inside, but she refused to let him know.

"Really?" Mr. Gatlin yanked her off the ground and held her in his face. "Then you might as well answer some questions! Where is the key?"

"What key?"

"The key! Any key!"

Maggie shivered. "I don't know."

Mr. Thomas Gatlin threw her to the ground. Maggie skidded across the dirt on her backside until she hit the bottom step of the porch. Gatlin strode over to tower above her. "Kid, this is not a game. I mean business. Sue has a key, and I want it. If you don't know where it is, you must have a good idea where she would keep it."

Maggie rubbed her head. "If you didn't find it when you tore up the house, then it probably isn't there."

"That boxcar?" he chuckled.

"It's our home." Maggie felt her heart swelling. It was her home, and she treasured it. She sure wished she were there right now.

"Where does Sue put her important papers?" He leaned in closer to Maggie.

Maggie trembled. "She put her marriage license in her Bible."

"That's a good start. So her important papers are in her Bible." Mr. Gatlin looked up at Stub. "You find that Bible with those papers in it?"

"Sure, boss, but … uh … I didn't think you was wantin' papers. I … I … thought you wanted a key. There weren't no key stashed in that … uh … holy book," Stub stuttered.

"It's got to be there." Gatlin ran his fingers threw his hair. He turned back to Maggie. "Surely you can think where a key would be."

"What kind of key?"

"That doesn't matter."

"It might. A person might hang a house key by the door. If it were a key to a car, a person might put it in the shed." Maggie explained.

Mr. Gatlin paused, his eyes narrowed. "It's a key to a safety deposit box."

Maggie swallowed. Mr. Thomas Gatlin had been in the bank trying to get Mr. Crenshaw to give him information about a safety deposit box. Mr. Crenshaw was willing to lose his job over keeping that information from him. After he left, Mr. Crenshaw had asked Maggie if Sue had important things. Maggie began to wonder if Sue did have important things. Maybe she had secrets Maggie didn't know about.

"Well, where would she keep a key like that?" Gatlin cut into her thoughts.

"With her money, but she doesn't have any money." Maggie shrugged.

Maybe Sue didn't know she had money. If she didn't, she wouldn't know the key was important. That was it! Sue had the key, but she didn't know it had more than sentimental value! Maggie's heart started beating faster. She gasped. She knew where the key was. They wouldn't have found it in the house. Opal wore it around her neck. Opal and Ruby's daddy had given it to Sue, and Sue had given it to Opal when she married Daddy. It was just a key. Opal called it, "a key to my heart and the secrets in it!" The key did hold secrets. Maggie bit her lower lip. She couldn't tell them. They would go grab Opal. That would be too horrible a thing to happen to Opal. Maggie wouldn't let that happen.

Mr. Thomas Gatlin turned to Maggie. "Did you remember something?"

Maggie shook her head.

Gatlin grabbed the double barrel from Stub, swung it around and aimed it at Maggie's head. "You better tell me what you just thought of!"

Maggie gasped for air. It felt like her lungs were exploding. They were over full of air, but she couldn't breathe. She wouldn't tell him about Opal.

Gatlin cocked the gun. The sound seemed to blast through Maggie's whole body. She jerked. She had to tell him something … anything! "I don't know anything about Sue. My daddy just married her at the beginning of the summer. I don't know where she would keep that key."

Gatlin shoved the barrel against her nose.

Maggie didn't know when the tears started spewing out of her. The double barrel fit over her nose like a pair of old lady spectacles, and that was probably the last sight on this earth she would ever see. "You have got to believe me!" she shouted.

Instead of pulling the trigger, Mr. Thomas Gatlin swung the gun like a baseball bat. Maggie's body seemed to burst, and she sprawled across the ground. From beyond time, Maggie heard Stub yelling, "You killed her! Boss, you killed her!" Then time was no more. There was only quiet piled upon silence.

Hours later Maggie rolled over and pulled her eyes open. Dust particles danced in the light rays that found their path through the slits in the roof. Where was she? Her head was splitting. Her tongue felt three sizes too big for her mouth. She wished for a drink of water. Water. This must be how the land felt since there had been no rain. She should try to sit up. Maybe that would tell her where she was. Maggie pushed her hands beneath her body and shoved. Her world spun. She thought she would throw up. She dropped her head to her knees and closed her eyes. Her mouth felt grainy. She sputtered. Tiny dirt clods flew into the flour sack material of her dress. "Eeww!" She had a mouth full of dirt. She badly needed a drink! Little trickles of sweat dribbled down her cheeks. The stuffy air smelled like something rotting. She had to find out where the men had put her. Again, she forced her eyes open and very slowly lifted her head. The room had a dirt floor. A couple of weeds had sprouted and died. Three or four buckets were strewn about. To the side a pile of dried corn built a small hill. Some crates just like the one the sheriff had found in their cow shed were stacked half way to the roof of the building. Maggie guessed if she were real thirsty she could get a drink from one of those bottles. Stub Huggins said moonshine was for medicinal purposes. Maggie's head felt like it needed some medicine. At first, Maggie didn't know if the building was round or if her eyes were playing tricks on her. She put her hands to the side of her head to steady it. Yes, the building was round like the granaries Daddy had on their farm. She hadn't seen any granaries, but then she hadn't looked around very much. Maggie gazed at the door. If she could get on her feet, maybe she could get out of here. She tried. Standing was pretty unsteady. Instead, she crawled over to the door. It had no handle! Maggie pulled herself up and lunged against it. The door didn't budge. She tried again.

Finally, she turned and leaned with her back on the wooden door and searched the rest of the building. Maybe she could find a loose board somewhere. There just had to be a way out. She slid down to the dirt floor. Thirst was killing her. Before long, she would be forced to take a drink from one of Stub's moonshine bottles. She tried to swallow. Slowly she crossed to the stack of crates. She needed something to pry it open. She searched the place. One of the bucket handles was loose. Maybe that would work. She picked up the wire handle and started trying to bend it, but it was too hard. She dropped it at her feet and bent over to rest her elbows on the top crate of the stack. She noticed the crate was just wired shut. Maggie struggled to get her fingers working. She twisted and yanked at the wire until she had one side open enough to squeeze a bottle out. Maggie held it in her hand and looked to the roof. "Dear God up in heaven, please forgive me, but I think I'm going to die if I don't get a drink of something!" Maggie pulled on the cork. It wouldn't budge. "That is probably God saving me from strong drink, moonshine and bootlegging. I'm really sorry, God!" Maggie stuck the end of the cork between her teeth and yanked. It popped and moonshine spewed over the sides and down Maggie's dress. "Well, I guess I'll smell like an old drunk," Maggie mumbled.

Maggie froze. What was that? Maggie held very still. She could hear hushed footsteps. Someone was coming! Slowly she stuck the cork back in the bottle and set it beside the pile of crates. She picked it up again. She would need a weapon! She tried to spring toward the door. The floor seemed to heave itself up and down. She grabbed her stomach to stop the retching feeling. Maggie moved to the wall by the door and flattened herself against it. She gripped the cold, hard moonshine bottle in her hand and waited. It would work, if she had enough energy to swing it. It would work. It had to work. Maggie raised it above her head and waited.

CHAPTER 14

Midnight Train

The footsteps stopped and Maggie could hear someone fumbling at the door. "Stupid wire!" A low voice spat. The door must have been wired shut. No wonder she couldn't open it. Whoever stood on the other side of the door was impatient. He gave it a hard whack and yanked the door open.

Maggie gritted her teeth and held the bottle high. She swung as hard as she could. The cork flew out of the bottle and moonshine doused her. The strong smelling liquid burned the gash in her head. The bottle slid from her hands and landed at Jed's feet.

Jed blinked. "Well, I guess you're alive." He bent over and picked up the bottle. "If you drink too much of this, you won't be for long!" He started to hand the bottle back to Maggie, but then yanked it away. "I'm s'posed to see if you're still alive."

Maggie swallowed. "Jed, what are they going to do with me?"

"I'm not s'posed to know." He kept between Maggie and the door.

"But you do know, don't you?"

Jed flipped the bottle in the air and caught it.

"What are they planning to do?" Maggie quietly asked. She could feel that Jed knew and maybe, just maybe he would help her. "Please, Jed, you have to let me know." Maggie tried to keep her voice even and calm.

He took a step farther into the stifling granary, turned, pulled the wire through the door and twisted it shut. He grabbed a couple of buckets and turned them upside down. He motioned for her to sit on one, and he sat on the other. Jed had trouble looking Maggie in the face.

"Jed, I need to know," Maggie pleaded.

"The boss was pretty sure you were already dead. He thought if you weren't, you might never be right in the head again." He pointed to her head. "It looks pretty bad. Hurt?"

Maggie nodded. She reached up to her head. She felt dried blood and a huge knot bursting through the split on her skull. It was very tender. Her head throbbed and her stomach must think it was flipping from ride to ride in an amusement park!

Maggie chewed on her bottom lip. "Did they want me dead?"

Jed slid his eyes toward her. "No. The boss just lost his temper. I think my pa is scared of him."

"Is that why your pa got me?" Maggie didn't want to use the word "kidnap."

Jed shrugged. "Pa ain't never been scared of anyone before, but when he thought the boss was gonna shoot you ..." Jed shook his head.

"Jed, what if you let me go?"

Jed stiffened. "I can't let you go."

"What if I just got away?"

Jed shook his head. "Pa's scared of the boss. I can't let you go. We'd lose the place and I'd get the beating of my life."

Maggie sighed. She was so thirsty. "Jed, can you get me some water?"

Jed stared at her. "I can, but I have to wire you in again."

Maggie nodded. So much for the idea of getting away while he got her water. She needed the water.

"I'll be back." Jed strode to the door and left. Maggie heard him wire the door.

She felt her head. At least the moonshine should have killed the germs. She smiled. God had saved her from drinking the moonshine. Maggie walked around the circle of the granary again and again. She was afraid to stay still. She might drift into a deep sleep or even pass out like before. Jed seemed to take forever, and her tongue was thick with thirst. She looked to the roof. Now it was past dusk outside. Some of the first stars were twinkling in the sky, and it would be really dark soon. That could make it easier to get away; then again, it might be harder.

"Hey, it's me." Jed tapped from the other side of the door.

Maggie crossed to the door and waited.

Jed stepped in. He handed Maggie the moonshine bottle. "It was easier to fill the bottle from the pump."

Maggie tipped it back and drank. The water trickled all the way down her throat. She thought it surely was the best water she had ever tasted.

Jed still stood in the doorway, fidgeting. He held the burlap sack.

Maggie's insides lurched to a stop. "What are you going to do with that?"

"I'm sorry." He closed the door and wired it shut.

"You going to kill me?" Maggie took a step back.

"I'm just s'posed to put you in the sack and tie it shut."

Maggie tried to search his eyes. She had heard of people putting kittens that they didn't want into a gunnysack, throwing the sack into water and drowning them! Was this what they planned to do with her? She put her hand over her beating heart and whispered. "Then what will you do?"

"I'm sorry! I'm sorry!"

"You're going to stick me in that sack and throw me into the water, aren't you?" Maggie threw her shoulders back and stood tall. She would not make it easy. She clutched the bottle in her fists. She would swing it with all her might.

Jed put a hand out. "No. They ain't gonna kill you. They pretty much think you're already dead. They're gonna throw the sack on the midnight train that goes back east. They think that's the best thing to do with the body."

"Why? Why do they think I'm dead?"

Jed scuffed at the dirt floor. "They think that 'cause I told them you was most already dead. I told them there was all your blood on the ground and you wouldn't move when I kicked you. They think there's no hope. That's why they want to stick your body on the midnight train. Before anyone finds it, it will be long gone from here."

"How do they plan to get me to the train?" Maggie's heart soared. She had Jed on her side.

"The boss is comin' about 11:00 tonight. They'll load you up. Then just east of Dodge, there's that big hill. The train goes almighty slow up that hill. That's when they're fixin' to throw the sack in an open car. I figure after that you can work your way out of the sack."

"What if I can't get out of the sack? What if someone throws me off the train? What if I get caught in the train wheels?" Maggie fought panic.

Jed rubbed the back of his neck with his hand. "I don't know. Wait." He dug in his pocket and pulled out a pocket-knife. "Here, this will help, but don't work out of that sack until you're on the train!"

"Thanks." Maggie took the knife and stared at Jed. "Do you know how much trouble your pa is in?"

"Plenty."

"He has kidnapped. People go to jail a long time for that. Your pa is not just going to lose his place. He's going to lose his whole lifetime with you. You'll be grown up when he gets out!"

"Pa didn't mean to kidnap you. People don't understand pa. He just wants to keep his place. That's all!"

"You want to keep him out of jail?" Maggie whispered.

"Sure, but I can't let you go."

"You don't have to."

"What would I have to do?"

"I know you can't slip away now, but what about after the boss loads me up? Could you go get help?"

"I ain't goin' to the police, if that's what you're gettin' at. That would be like turnin' in my own pa!"

Maggie nodded. "Okay, what about just going to some-where close? Maybe you could slip a message under the door or something where no one would even see you."

"I don't know."

Already the sky was getting dark. Jed seemed to be searching the roof for answers. He spread his hands wide. "I gave you the knife. I can't promise anything else." He looked at Maggie. His eyes slid away, but not before Maggie saw a tear rounding to fall.

"Okay, Jed." Maggie didn't want to push him too far. He was the only help she had.

Jed watched the floor. "I got to put you in the sack now."

"Now?" Chills exploded from her body. Maggie's very being wanted to yell, and shout, and run, but she had no place to go.

"If I don't turn up pretty soon, Pa will come lookin' for me. Then they'll know how alive you are. Do you want them to know?" Jed asked.

Violently Maggie shook her head, and then wished she hadn't. Everything was spinning and her tummy was retching again.

"Look, it's nigh dark now. The boss will be here before long, and it'll be better if he don't have to see nothin' but the sack." Jed's eyes begged her to agree.

"Okay, Jed." Maggie looked at the wadded up burlap. "Would you let me go in feet first? I thought I would die when your pa shoved it over my head and carried me upside down."

"Sure ... uh ..."

Maggie smiled. Jed didn't even know her name. "Maggie."

"Maggie," he whispered. "It's a nice name. It was my ma's name."

"It was my mama's name, too. I'm named for her," Maggie smiled. A long silence followed. Neither one seemed to know what to say.

Finally, Jed pushed the bag toward Maggie. "We'd best get on with it."

Maggie touched his hand and felt him tense. "Thank you, Jed. You are saving my life!"

"That girlie come back to life?" Stub called from somewhere outside.

Maggie jumped into the bag and struggled to pull it over her head.

"It's just harder than I thought to get her all stuck inside the bag!" Jed yelled over his shoulder while he wrapped the piece of rope around the top of the bag and tied it.

"I'll come give you a hand. That dead weight is hard to work with."

"Maggie, you got to heap up on the ground," Jed urged through clamped teeth.

Maggie quickly dropped.

Stub stepped into the granary. Maggie felt him grab the tied mouth of the gunnysack and pull it a couple of times. "Looks like you done real good, son. Here, give me a hand, and we'll haul it on out. The boss will be here before long."

Stub grabbed the front end of the bag. Jed took the back end. Maggie swayed back and forth as they carried her out of the granary.

"Let's drop it next to the porch," Stub told Jed.

"Okay, Pa."

The bag landed on the hard ground. Maggie sucked in her breath, as a rock jabbed her in the side. She badly wanted to move and find a more comfortable place, but she didn't dare. Stub thought she was dead, and dead people don't move. The burlap made her itch. She couldn't scratch. She felt the old, red hound sniff the bag and whine.

"Get away from there, you stupid dog!" Stub yelled and he must have thrown a rock because the hound yelped. The dog didn't leave. He snuggled beside the bag and started chewing on Maggie's foot through the burlap. Maggie tried to inch away. The dog chewed harder. Maggie gritted her teeth. She was ready to bite back!

"Come on, Bert." Jed's voice sifted through the sack. "You got to stay away from the bag."

Maggie could tell that Bert didn't want to go. Jed had to drag him. Maggie felt so thankful, she mumbled, "God up in heaven, thank you for Jed!"

"Pa, you want I should tie Bert to the porch so's he'll leave things alone?" Maggie heard Jed ask.

"Naw, it looks like the boss is a comin' now. That's him turnin' up the lane."

The motor got louder as the car chugged along the lane. The louder it got, the louder Maggie thought her heart pounded. Panic started pumping through her veins. What if Jed had lied to her? Her eyes flew open. What if they were really going to throw her into the river? The river was low, but it wouldn't take much to drown a person tied in a bag. There were cow tanks. They could throw her in one of those. Maggie had to stop thinking this way. She closed her eyes and made her body go limp. Jed. Jed wanted to help her. She would be fine. The God up in heaven loved her. He wouldn't let anything happen to her.

The auto stopped, but the engine continued to run. Maggie heard footsteps come close to her. "She dead?"

"Yep," Stub answered.

"You sure?"

Maggie held back a yelp as Stub poked her with some-thing, probably his double barrel. Maggie had never seen him without it.

"Load her up." Mr. Thomas Gatlin ordered.

"Come help me, boy," Stub called Jed.

Again, they raised Maggie into the air, carried her to the back of the car and dumped her into the trunk. The lid slammed, shutting Maggie in the trunk of the Hudson. It felt like a grave. She was buried alive. Maggie clutched Jed's pocketknife, trying to decide if she should cut her way out of the gunnysack right now. Why wait until they threw her on the train? Yet, if she cut the gunnysack while she was locked in the trunk of Mr. Gatlin's car, she would still be caught. No, she had to wait until she was on the train, away from Stub and Mr. Gatlin.

The Hudson turned and went down the bumpy road. If Maggie thought she'd been sick before, she hadn't known what sick was. Her head bounced against the metal bottom of the trunk until she sank into a black space between life and death. There were moments when she wanted to live and moments she wanted to die. It would be easier to give up. Surely heaven was better than this. Mama would be there. Yet, if she died, she would be giving up. Mr. Thomas Gatlin would win. Mr. Stub Huggins would get to keep his place. Daddy would miss her. Sue would miss her, and Opal and Ruby would, too. They might never even know what happened to her. No. She couldn't give up. She wouldn't give up. What was that song Mama used to sing? Or had it been Sue? Maggie smiled. Either way, it was Mama. "Again I faced Satan this morning. I battled him all the day long. At noon time God sent reinforcements and at sun-down I sang victory's song!" No. She wouldn't give up! "And the sun's coming up in the morning. Every tear will be gone from my eye! This old clay's gonna give way to glory, and like an eagle I'll take to the skies!" Maggie didn't even know that she sang out loud.

The car screeched to a stop.

Maggie hushed.

"What was that?" Stub yelled.

"What was what?" Gatlin asked.

"You didn't hear nothin'?"

"No."

"No singin'?"

"And just who would be singing?"

Maggie heard Stub whisper, "Angels! Lord have mercy!"

"Stub Huggins, you listen to me and you listen to me well. You are not going to go crazy on me. Not now. Not ever! We are here. The train is coming. We are going to throw this … this … bag on the train and then we are never going to speak of this again. Is that understood?"

Maggie could feel both men sweating, and that made her happy.

The train whistle blew. Maggie gasped with relief. Jed was right. It would be the train and not the river.

Someone yanked the trunk of the Hudson open. Maggie felt a rush of fresh air gush in. Both men grabbed the ends of the bag and tugged to get it out of the trunk. They dropped it to the ground, and someone— probably Stub—drug it to the edge of the tracks. Maggie hoped they didn't get too close.

Gatlin shouted above the roar of the train. "Stub, here comes an open car! It might be the only one, so we got to aim for it!"

Maggie felt them lift the gunnysack and start swinging.
"On the count of three, let go! One! Two! Three!"
Maggie felt like she had jumped out of a swing until she landed.

CHAPTER 15

Secrets Come Home

*T*HUD!!!!

Maggie moaned. She was dizzy. For a moment she lay still. The rhythmic noise and sway of the railroad car could lull her to sleep. Her whole body hurt so badly that sleep might be a nice release. Where would she be when she woke up? Who would there be to help her? No. She couldn't sleep. She had to get out of this sack. Maggie yanked open the pocketknife she had clutched in her hand and jabbed it through the burlap.

"Eeeow!"

Wildly Maggie began stabbing. Some bum was out there and she was stuck in this cocoon bag. She was helpless. She had to get out of this gunnysack.

"Maggie! Stop stabbing!" someone yelled. "We are trying to help you."

Maggie knew the voice, but the chugging train and burlap muffled the sound. Maggie held still. She didn't put away her knife. Some voices she knew were good, and some were bad.

She heard someone drop to the floor beside the bag and start untying the rope. Maggie gulped the fresh air that gushed into the bag. She flung her arms out and pulled the burlap away from her head. Maggie's mouth fell open. "Cecil? What? How did you get here?"

"I'll explain that later, but if you can, we need to get off this train fast. We're about to the top of the hill, and then we're going to fly down the other side. We won't be able to jump until we come to another hill. Do you think you can do it now?"

"Maggie can do anything."

"Elbert? You are here, too?"

"Maggie, we got to hurry!" Cecil yelled.

Maggie stripped off the bag and jumped to her feet. The car rocked and her head swam. Cecil and Elbert were pulling her to the open door of the railroad car. Maggie looked down at the passing gravel and froze. The wind tore at her clothes. The very skin of her face felt like it was being yanked away from her bones.

"Maggie, we got to do it! There's the top of the hill! The next hill might be miles from Dodge City!" Cecil shouted over the roar of the train and shook her arm.

Maggie nodded, but her body still wouldn't budge.

Cecil yelled over Maggie to Elbert. "Elbert, when I say 'GO,' dive out. Don't let go of Maggie's hand. We got to get her out of here before we go over that hill!"

Elbert grabbed Maggie's hand in a death grip and nodded. "GO!"

Both boys jumped, dragging Maggie with them. Maggie kicked as if she were swimming through the air. With a thud, they hit the ground and rolled. The train surged on. The earth vibrated. Cecil groaned from the bottom of the pile. Elbert giggled from the top. "That was grand! I can't wait to do it again."

"You're nuts, Elbert," Maggie murmured as she lay smashed between the two boys.

"Get off of me." Cecil grumbled.

Elbert rolled off the top and helped Maggie.

The train sped by and disappeared over the hill. It whistled as if saying goodbye and rumbled into the night. Quiet settled in. A few fireflies blended with the stars twinkling above. Crickets chattered to each other and Maggie drew in cool, Kansas night air. She was alive. The three sat in a circle and looked at each other.

Maggie broke the silence. "How did you know I was on that train?"

"Jed."

"You know Jed?"

"I know him now." Cecil studied Maggie. "He wanted to help you awful bad. He said you were too nice to end up the way the boss had planned." Cecil paused. "Maggie, who is the boss?"

Maggie furrowed her brows. "I have to talk to Daddy first before I tell anyone."

"Okay. Maggie you look awful. Do you think you can walk? It's over a mile to your house." Cecil kept watching Maggie.

"I can walk. I might be slow, but I can do it." Maggie pulled herself to her feet.

"Maggie, Jed didn't tell us much about what happened. You're all bloody. How did you get that way?"

"You been gone all day." Elbert added. "Everybody has been looking for you."

"I've been gone only a day? It feels like I've been gone more than a week." Maggie mumbled. She started following the tracks. The tracks passed her boxcar house, the one place she wanted to be. Cecil and Elbert swung along beside her.

Cecil picked up a stick and used it like a staff. "The sheriff was checking our cellar when Jed came. I guess they thought maybe Aunt Louise had shut you down there again."

Maggie shivered at the thought of the cellar.

Cecil laughed. "Aunt Louise threw a hissy fit. She told the sheriff she would have him arrested. Can you imagine that? Arrest the sheriff."

"Uncle Arnold cried. I ain't never seen Uncle Arnold cry," Elbert added.

"Yep. He cried. He kept telling Aunt Louise if she had anything to do with you being gone he would leave her. She pranced around and told him to go on and take out. She would just go live with her cousin, Thomas Gatlin! She said she was tired of the fuss Uncle Arnold made over just a ..." Cecil seemed to be looking for the word he wanted.

"Little bit of a tramp! That's what Aunt Louise called Maggie." Elbert slung a rock at the track. It hit, and the twang echoed into the night.

"Elbert, I wasn't going to tell Maggie that." Cecil thumped his head.

"Well, that's what she said."

"It's okay." Maggie shrugged. "She's called me that before." Maggie wasn't a bit surprised. She felt sorry for Mr. Crenshaw. He'd been really nice to her when Mrs. Crenshaw hadn't.

"I tried to get Jed to tell the sheriff because he was right there, but he wouldn't budge. He just kept saying he would probably get the beating of his life as it was. We would have at least gotten Uncle Arnold, but Jed told us we didn't have time. If we missed the midnight train, we would miss you. So we cut across your pasture and the Gatlin back pasture. We just made it in time!" Cecil was still full of excitement.

"I was scared jumping on the train." Elbert whistled. "If Cecil hadn't grabbed me when he did, I would have gone under the wheels!" Elbert swiped his forehead as if remembering made him sweat.

Maggie stopped. She turned to Cecil and looked him in the eye. "Cecil, I didn't think you liked me. Wouldn't this have been an easy way you could have gotten even with me? You promised you would get even. Remember?"

Cecil poked his walking stick in the ground. "Aw, Maggie. You bring good stuff to us every day."

Maggie smiled and whispered. "Mrs. Valina's heaping coals."

Cecil looked past Maggie at nothing. "It's more fun when you are around. You get mad at us sometimes, but mostly you are happy, even when Aunt Louise treats you terrible."

Elbert tugged at Maggie's arm and whispered. "He got the God up in heaven in his heart."

Maggie stopped and looked at Elbert. "How?"

Elbert shrugged. "He asked me. I told him. I hope I done right."

Maggie looked Cecil up and down.

Shyly Cecil turned to gaze at the sky. "Mighty dark," he said.

"It seems to have taken. Elbert, you did just fine."

Maggie's face broke out in a smile. "Thanks, Cecil."

Cecil pointed with his stick. "I see lights in your house. Your mama and daddy must still be up."

Maggie's heart soared. That was the best sight ever. She wanted to run, but her legs and head wouldn't let her. She was ready to fall on the spot.

Cecil noticed. "Want a piggyback ride?"

Maggie giggled. "I think I'm too big!"

Cecil laughed. "I'll bet you're not! Elbert, help her get up."

Maggie was too tired to argue. She must have passed out because the next thing she knew, Daddy carried her in the house saying her name over and over again. He sat in the rocker still holding her.

"Sam, we've got to get her to the doctor." Sue clapped her hand over her mouth. Tears streamed down her face.

Ruby sobbed.

Opal shook her fist at Cecil. "If you did this to her, I'll clean your plow!"

Maggie giggled. She loved Opal and Ruby, but as much as she would like to see Opal do just that, she intervened. "Opal, he didn't do it. He helped me."

Opal still glared at Cecil. "If she's hurt, and I find out you did it, you are still going to get it!"

Sue stepped in. "Opal, he helped Maggie. He carried her here, so be nice to him. Tell him you are sorry," Sue ordered.

"Sorry." Opal stuck her tongue out when her mother wasn't looking, and mouthed the words, "Just wait …"

Cecil smiled and shoved one fist into the other.

"Opal?" Maggie remembered. "Do you still have the key to your heart?"

Opal crossed to Maggie and reached for her hand. "Yes, why?"

"It is a key to secrets!"

Opal's eyes sparkled. "Secrets? Is it worth a lot of money, like treasure?"

"What?" Sue whispered.

"Is that what someone tore up our house for?" Opal asked in awe. She pulled her key from beneath her nightgown and kissed it.

Ruby crowded close. "It's not just an old dumb key?"

Maggie shook her head. "No, Ruby, it's not just an old dumb key."

Opal leaned closer to Maggie. "Maggie, what is the treasure?"

Maggie shrugged. "I don't know what the treasure is, but I know where the treasure is." Maggie felt like she would burst. She knew something that Opal wanted to know so badly. She wanted to watch her squirm just a little longer.

"Where is it?" Opal wanted to shout.

"Maggie?" Sue asked.

"The key goes to a safety deposit box at the bank."

Sue sank to the floor. "Albert knew! He knew the day he was killed! We stopped by the gas station that day. He was so excited. Sam, he gave me this key. He said it was the key to his heart, and it held secrets that would change our life. He told me he couldn't wait until after work. He said he wanted to tell me in a very special way." Sue whispered, "Then there was the fire and he never came home!"

Opal still held the key. Gently she pulled it over her neck and held it out to Sue. Sue looked at the key nestled in the chubby palm of Opal's hand. Maggie thought it wasn't just the key she saw. It was memories of Albert.

"Maggie," Daddy tipped her chin to look into his eyes. "Who did this to you? Who wanted the key?"

"Mostly it was Mr. Thomas Gatlin. He is the boss. Stub Huggins helped him because Mr. Gatlin told him he could keep his place if he helped."

"I should have known!"

"Sam," Sue interrupted. "I think someone is here."

"Sue, get the gun." Daddy rose from the rocker with Maggie.

A car door slammed. "Daniels!" A pounding sounded from the porch door.

Elbert twisted the tail of his shirt. "That's Uncle Arnold!"

"Daniels, someone took my nephews, too!" Maggie could hear the worry in his voice.

"Boy, are we in trouble." Cecil looked to the ceiling.

Elbert hid behind Cecil.

Sue swung the door open. "They are in here, Mr. Crenshaw. Come on in."

Mr. Crenshaw mopped his head. He stooped in front of the boys. "Are you okay?"

"They helped me, Mr. Crenshaw," Maggie spoke.

He turned, seeing Maggie for the first time. "They found you!" The color drained from his face. "Oh! What happened to you? I'll drive you to the doctor."

Daddy was grim. "Arnold, you would have to drive all of us. I will not leave any of my family here without me. Too many things have happened and still could happen."

"It'll be a squeeze, but we can do it." He turned to the boys, "Come on boys. You made me proud by helping Maggie. You boys can tell me all about it on the way."

Outside, the eastern sky blushed.

Mr. Crenshaw, Sue and Daddy with Maggie on his lap snuggled in the front seat of the car. Sue scrunched her knees to the side of the gearshift. They were more crowded than the kids in the back seat. Opal especially complained about sitting against Cecil. Elbert dove between the two of them and Opal liked it less. Maggie smiled. She thought Opal really had a crush on Cecil.

As the car puttered down the dusty road, the story poured out. Mr. Crenshaw tapped his fingers on the steering wheel. "That key must have been given to your husband by the lawyer who visited me at the bank that day. I wondered whom he gave it to. He was from out of town. He wanted a safety deposit box and the only comment he made was that the contents would rock the very foundation of Dodge City. I never found out who got the key, and no one ever came into the bank with it to open the box. It's been quite a mystery. I'll tell you what we'll do. After the doctor gets done with Maggie, we'll head to the bank and open that safety deposit box!"

Maggie couldn't stand it. "Please, can't we just go to the bank first?"

"No. Maggie you need taken care of. You are more important than whatever might be in that locked box," Daddy told her.

"But, Daddy, what if the doctor won't let me go? Really I am fine, and I want to see what is in that box!" Maggie could see him waver. "PLEASE?"

"I don't know. Sue, what do you think?"

Maggie clasped Sue's hand. "Please, Mama!"

Sue smiled. "I think Maggie will be fine. After all, she's waited this long, and Dr. Nelson won't be up yet."

They drove along the quiet streets of Dodge City until the sedan crunched to a stop in front of the bank. Everyone piled out. They surrounded Mr. Crenshaw and held their breath as he fumbled with the key. When the door swung wide, Maggie felt like an intruder stepping into the dark bank. Mr. Crenshaw took them to his office to wait while he went to the vault. No one broke the silence. Maggie could hear the vault door grind, and found she was counting Mr. Crenshaw's footsteps as he came back. "Now, Sue, would you like us to leave the room? Legally, it is your right to open the box by yourself if you wish."

Sue rested her eyes on the box. She caressed the key. "No, Albert was a wonderful part of my life. He gave me Opal and Ruby." She turned to Sam. "You are a wonderful part of my life now. You have given me Margaret Pearl. I want all of my family to share this moment with me."

Daddy still held Maggie. He reached over and laid his hand on Sue's. Maggie could feel the glow between them.

"Very well. Boys, let's give them their privacy." Mr. Crenshaw set the box on his desk.

"No. Mr. Crenshaw, please stay." Sue handed him the key. "Will you open it for me?"

"Are you sure?"

Sue nodded.

Mr. Crenshaw stuck the key in the lock and turned. He flipped the lid up and took out a brown envelope. He handed it to Sue.

"That's it? An old dumb envelope?" Opal huffed.

"No treasure?" Ruby's bottom lip hung.

Sue opened the envelope and pulled out a wad of legal papers. She looked at them, then to Mr. Crenshaw. "Would you interpret these for us? It has been a long night!"

Mr. Crenshaw smiled. "I'll see how good I am at reading legal documents." He walked behind his desk and sat while he scanned the papers, every now and again turning pages. A smile grew. He seemed to forget everyone else in the room. He flew through the pages. Finally, he folded them and tapped them on the edge of his desk. He looked up with a twinkle in his eye.

"Well?" Sue asked.

"Sue did you know much of Albert's past?" Mr. Crenshaw asked.

"His mother raised him. After she died, he had no family."

Mr. Crenshaw smiled. "It seems his real last name was Gatlin."

"What?" Sue gasped. "How?"

"Thomas Gatlin Sr. met and married an army nurse stationed in France. Then military orders separated them, and they lost all communication with each other. Eventually, the military notified Mr. Gatlin Sr. that his wife was no longer living, and not knowing they had a son, he stopped searching for her. Albert's mother located Mr. Gatlin Sr. sometime after he had remarried, but she never contacted him because she didn't want to intrude on his new life. Shortly before his death, Mr. Gatlin Sr. learned of his son, Albert, and he left Albert half of the Gatlin estate."

Sue blinked in surprise.

"You are a very wealthy woman, Sue." Mr. Crenshaw smiled.

"It is a treasure!" Opal jumped up and down. She grabbed Ruby and swung her in circles.

The outer door crashed. "See! I told you someone broke into the bank!"

Maggie knew that voice. She jumped from Daddy's lap and hid behind his chair. Her heart pounded.

Mr. Thomas Gatlin stormed into the office and stopped in front of Daddy. He pointed. "I might have known it was you breaking into the bank! A thief! Sheriff, arrest this man!"

"Whoa, Thomas, he doesn't look like he is robbing the bank to me." The sheriff stuck his thumbs in his belt loops.

"Then just what is he doing in the bank at this hour?"

"Ask him."

"You're the sheriff. You ask him! Besides being in the bank, he's a known bootlegger!" Gatlin sputtered.

"How would you know that, Thomas?" The sheriff asked.

"I have inside information, but if you want proof, just go out to his place and snoop around. I'll bet you find moonshine!" Gatlin roared.

"My daddy is not a bootlegger!" Maggie stood from behind the chair.

Mr. Thomas Gatlin's face turned gray. "Angels! Stub heard angels!" He backed away.

Maggie walked around the chair to stand in front of Mr. Thomas Gatlin. Her hair was matted with blood from the split gouged in her head. Dried blood clung to the side of her face and down her crumpled dress. Maggie poked Mr. Gatlin in the chest. "He didn't hear angels. He heard me. You are going to hear me now. My daddy is not a bootlegger. He is a good man. He has the fruit of the spirit in him. You don't. You kidnapped me. You hit me. You almost shot me with Stub Huggins' scattergun. You threw me on a train headed out of town!"

Daddy came from behind Maggie and scooped her up before she collapsed. Gently he handed her to Sue.

The sheriff took his handcuffs from his belt. "Kidnapping, Thomas?"

"She's right here! She can't be kidnapped if she is here!"

The sheriff looked at Maggie. "Did you go with this man by choice?"

"No! I was stuffed in a gunnysack!"

The sheriff nodded. "That makes it kidnapping." A slow smile spread across his face. "Sam, do you want to do the honors?"

"I sure would!" He took the handcuffs from the sheriff. "Mr. Thomas Gatlin, you are under arrest for the kidnapping of Margaret Pearl Daniels, my," he paused and looked at Sue, "our daughter," he corrected.

Gatlin jerked his hands away. "You can't do that! Only the sheriff can!"

"And Sam," the sheriff winked. "Sam Daniels. Meet my deputy!"

"Meet my Daddy!" Maggie added.

"I'll have your job!" Gatlin raged.

The sheriff scrunched his brows together in thought. "I don't know that prisoners can vote, Mr. Gatlin."

Everyone in the room laughed, except Mr. Thomas Gatlin.

Don't miss
After the Dust Settles
Book 4 in the Gatlin Fields Series
Available now!

A secret pain that only love can heal

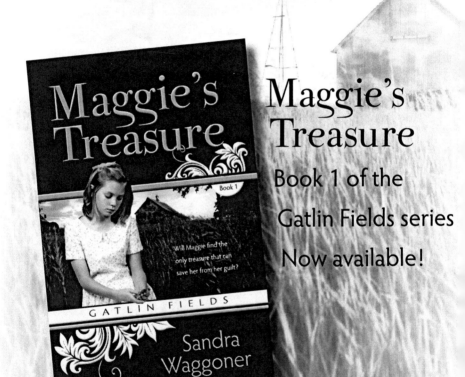

Maggie's Treasure

Book 1 of the

Gatlin Fields series

Now available!

CPSIA information can be obtained at www.ICGtesting.com
Printed in the USA
LVOW10s0920091213

364494LV00002B/9/P